I0780885

Published by: Cinnabar Moth Publishing LLC
Santa Fe, New Mexico

Cover Design by: Ira Geneve

ISBN-13: 978-1-962308-27-4

Library of Congress Control Number: 2024948035

Kinetics

NATHANIEL KOSZER

CHAPTER ONE

"So how do you feel? And I need you to be honest with me," Symon asked.

"No pain. Honestly. Not from the jaw, not from my arm and not from the ribs," Nadine replied.

Symon sighed. "Okay, I believe you. You are cleared for takeoff," he said with a smirk.

As soon as Symon uttered those words, Nadine took to the air and screamed at the top of her lungs. She started doing laps above Heinz field, circling ever higher and farther outward. From the second Nadine had learned to fly, every takeoff had been for a purpose: fighting Spidre's peacekeeper soldiers, saving Edgar so she could confess her love, escaping an ambush, playing her part in bringing down the Net Tower and crippling the military's communications. Add to that an additional six weeks of being grounded due to injuries from the net tower assault, and it all made this into a moment of complete ecstasy for her. She hoped to follow this celebratory flight with a celebratory fight, but when she looked south, where the peacekeepers had decided to attack today, she could see them in retreat at the hands of Edgar, Naren, and Victor.

As much as she wanted to get involved, she knew that if they had it under control, then strategically speaking she was more useful waiting at Heinz field in case another attack came from somewhere else. Spidre's army had tried this strategy many times while she was recovering, and on a few occasions they'd almost succeeded. So she descended back to the field, toward a lonely orange glow at the northeast corner. It was Sera. She was awake but lying down on a mattress with a bunch of pillows propping up her back.

"Glad to see you didn't forget how to fly!" Sera joked as Nadine landed next to her.

Nadine chuckled. "I spent 26 years trying to get off the ground. You are all lucky I ever came back down."

Sera smiled. "So, four of us are back in fighting shape, only one to go," she said.

"You'll be throwing peacekeepers around soon enough," Nadine said. "The rest of us only had bullet holes, burns, broken bones, normal stuff. You practically cooked your insides holding all that energy to explode the base of the net tower. The fact that you're even able to heal from something like that shows how strong you are."

"I know, I know," Sera replied. "I just really want to get the next phase of the plan moving."

"You mean kicking Spidre's army out of New Orleans?" Nadine asked.

"Wait, we didn't talk about that yet, how did…? You know what, never mind. Of course you figured the plan out," Sera replied as she shook her head.

"I understand that desire, it's your hometown! Hell, I wanted to liberate Chicago for the same reason," Nadine said.

"It just fucking sucks!" Sera exclaimed. "We fought our asses off to destroy the androids, and the second they're gone, Spidre moves another army right in! When we heard the news after taking over Gibraltar, I had to fight with all my willpower to keep myself from flying back over the ocean and thrashing them."

"The time for thrashing will come, don't worry," Nadine said with a smirk.

Outside the stadium, past the Ohio river and the destroyed bridges that dotted its banks, Victor was a blur as he raced between ancient crumbling buildings. He was looking up, towards the sky. Even on a clear day like today, the bright blue streak of light that Naren left as he flew was unmistakable. With the fighting over, Victor knew that if he followed Naren, they would eventually find and regroup with Edgar. Sure enough, a short time later, Naren began to descend. When Victor turned to meet him, he saw Edgar directly below Naren's downward path.

"I hate when they attack from this side," Edgar said as Naren and Victor came within earshot. Seeing them, Edgar knew the fight must be over, and he withdrew the blue blades of raw energy that had been projecting from his hands.

"Why?" Naren asked Edgar.

"With all the bridges destroyed, we can't get any of the big, mounted guns over to our side and use them. It's annoying!" Edgar replied.

"I assume that's why they do it," Naren said. "Look at what happened in the North. Every time they tried to get through, they failed, and each time they gave us more equipment to use. Now we're so heavily fortified there the locals can fight off huge amounts of peacekeepers with ease."

"I actually don't mind when they attack from this side," Victor said. "It gives us more to do. We have to destroy the heavy guns so the peacekeepers can't take them back, and we have to bring the small guns and lasers over to our side. I'd much rather do that than go back and do Symon's stupid tests."

"*Here we go again,*" Edgar thought to himself.

"Like, I get it. I overloaded on energy, and it was bad. But it took years for that to happen! We don't have to worry about it for a long time!" Victor continued.

"I don't think we know that for sure," Naren said.

"What do you mean?" Victor asked.

"Well, think about it: The LO-EC technology in our body is designed to turn excess body heat from physical exertion into useable bioenergy. That energy is stored in the micro-transformers that are supposed to be in the palms of our hands. But the LO-EC tech in your body isn't like that. It's creating incredible amounts of energy and giving you your powers, but the lone micro-transformer you have can't keep up. The more you exert yourself, the more of that energy is just jostling around inside you. When you were alone in the woods all those years, you only used your speed when you had to to survive. You weren't physically exerting yourself like you have been these past few months.

"So…" Victor replied.

"So, that energy buildup didn't take years, most of it happened since you met us. Or at least that's what Symon thinks, and he is the expert here. And I think describing what happened as simply 'overloading on energy' is a bit understated. You nearly died, Victor. You were closer to death than any of us have ever come. Think about that. All of us were in hiding for twenty years from a world that wanted us dead. Sera and I cared for her religious followers in secret from three ruthless androids that would have killed us without hesitation. Nadine, Edgar, and Symon not only survived a tussle with the most powerful commander in the military, but also held off a direct assault from Spidre, the literal world leader and a secretly powerful LO-EC. And then when we were finally all united, we fought and defeated the androids, then traveled the world directly confronting the world's army multiple times, culminating with a fight in New York with an army likely numbering in the millions. And yet, the closest any of us came to dying was you on that day in Monaco, with the peacekeepers scarcely laying a finger on you. Your power is incredible, Victor, but it's also the biggest threat to your safety."

"Well then why the fuck am I fighting, Naren?!" Victor yelled. "If fighting this much is making me go through all this shit and is going to kill me, then why don't I just go back to hiding in the woods!?"

"We're fighting so that you don't have to hide in the fucking woods!" Edgar exclaimed in reply. The outburst seemed to snap Victor back to reality.

"He's right," Naren said. "I don't think your hideout is safe anyway. After we destroyed the androids, the peacekeepers almost certainly searched the forest and probably found your camp. But, regardless, none of us plan to fight forever. This will end, we will have peace. So, for now, deal with Symon's examinations so that you can live to see that day."

Victor huffed but nodded in agreement.

"Ok. Victor, can you start finding the dead soldiers and stripping their BEOS weapons and armor? I'll go back overhead to find the heavy artillery and point Edgar towards it," Naren said.

With that, everyone nodded and went about their assigned tasks. Edgar went wherever Naren directed from the air and sliced up the heavy weaponry while Victor started stripping bodies. When he had collected several armfuls, Victor got them back to Heinz field using the trick he had learned in New York: After building up some speed on land, Victor leapt off the shoreline and continued running over the surface of the Ohio river. After several trips, there didn't appear to be any more weapons or armor worth carrying, so he went back to Heinz field. There, Symon was waiting to check his vitals and make sure nothing was out of the ordinary. A few minutes later, Naren also returned to the field with Edgar dangling from his arms. Every time she saw this, Sera couldn't help but chuckle. It was silly looking, but it got the job done.

"So…" Edgar said to Nadine as he landed.

"I'm flying again!" Nadine exclaimed. Edgar pumped his fist in celebration and the two rushed to meet each other and embrace. As they did so, Naren unclipped something from his waistband. It was a black rectangular box about twice the size of the military-issued mobiles which, thanks to their actions in New York, no longer worked.

"They had more of these today. What did you call them again?" Naren asked.

"Radios," Symon replied. "Hard to believe such ancient technology is what the world's army has to resort to."

"And did you finish taking apart the one they found the other day? Did you find out if they're only short-range communication?" Nadine asked as she and Edgar ended their embrace.

"I took it apart, and I think it's short-range only, but I'm not entirely sure," Symon said. "I know radios certainly can be used long distance. Hell, back in the day, they used to use radios to communicate with literal spaceships going to other planets. But I don't think these are those. The power supply is tiny. If I had to put a number on it, I'd say these can be a mile or two from each other, at most. And they aren't being mass produced. These are being made by hand somewhere by someone who happens to know radio technology."

"So the whole military might not have them yet, just the ones around here," Naren said. "But there is no telling when they'll spread and when they'll develop the longer-range radios. We need to…"

Naren's thought was cut off by a sound that filled everyone with dread. Before the LO-ECs had come to Pittsburgh, the rebelling locals had started building an air raid siren at the top of their megaskyscraper, just in case it was ever needed. It was only used once, during testing, once it was finished. The LO-ECs had heard it while they were recovering from their battle in New York. Now, weeks later, they were hearing it again. Their eyes trained to the sky, where against the light blue about two dozen black dots congregated.

"Push them off course!" Symon yelled as Naren grabbed Victor and flew full speed to the top of the megaskyscraper. Victor appreciated the lift, as the only other viable option was the megaskyscraper elevator, and that enclosed space frightened him far more than any missile. When Naren dropped Victor off, he turned to see Nadine had taken off as well and was heading straight towards the incoming missiles. Naren again took off like a shot and, being the fastest flyer, was the first to reach the missiles. When he did, he swung around to try and match their speed downward. In the panic of the moment, it was difficult to judge how hard to hit the missile without blowing it up, but he went for it. The middle didn't explode, only briefly went off course before somehow correcting itself and returning to its trajectory.

How did it do that?! he thought to himself. *The net tower is down, any sort of targeting network shouldn't be working.*

He tried again and again, hitting the missile harder this time, but it was the same result. By now, Nadine had joined in and was trying to knock another missile off its path with no success. From his perch, Victor threw air burst after air burst, desperately trying to knock the missiles away, but even that was no good. Every time a missile was diverted, it righted itself again. Frustrated, Victor threw multiple air bursts in succession, causing one missile to slam into the other, exploding them both. Seeing success, he tried doing the same thing again, but the remaining missiles were spread too far apart. He could briefly push them, but it was not enough.

This doesn't make sense! Nadine thought to herself as she yet again unsuccessfully pushed against a missile. If she kept contact with it for an extended period of time, she could keep putting it farther and farther off course, but it fought her the whole time. She imagined she could push one far enough away that it wouldn't hit the field or the rebel-controlled area, but that left twenty other missiles they could do nothing about. She couldn't simply punch through the shell, either. She might hit the missile controls, but she might also hit the explosives.

As she struggled against her metal foe, she glanced down at the stadium and saw something new. On the outside of the facade was a tiny but brilliantly bright point of light.

What the fuck is that?! she thought, and then immediately had an idea. She pushed the nose of the missile to the right, and sure enough the missile pointed itself back toward the point of light.

Did the peacekeepers put that light on the building somehow?! she continued to think to herself. *No, that doesn't make any sense. It must be projected from somewhere else. But where… there!*

Nadine's attempts to divert the missile had brought her relatively close to a hilly area just outside of the main city. As her eyes darted around, she caught sight of a lone peacekeeper looking towards Heinz field and holding another light that looked like the one on the stadium's side. She abandoned the missile and careened down towards the peacekeeper. The peacekeeper was so focused on his task that he didn't see Nadine until the moment she slammed into him, driving him into the dirt so hard that his armor and bones shattered into pieces. When she made contact, the light on the side of the stadium went out, and suddenly Naren was met with far less resistance pushing the missile. Nadine took off to meet up with the missiles again, but from her perspective she could see plain as day they weren't going to make it. Victor could push some of the missiles but not all of them, and she and Naren just wouldn't be able to make up the difference.

As Nadine began to fill with a host of negative emotions, they were immediately swept away by the sight of Sera's orange glow hurdling into the sky. Victor saw this and immediately knew what he had to do. He started throwing air bursts in rapid succession again, trying to get the missiles bunched together as close as possible. As Sera reached the right height, she unleashed her explosive energy, sending a blue shockwave out in every direction. Most of the missiles exploded immediately. The few that didn't were knocked far off course and into the fields of abandoned buildings left from before the megaskyscrapers were constructed.

I… don't feel good, Sera thought to herself. Letting off her blast wasn't the problem. She had to do that twice a day every day, whether injured or not. It was flying so quickly and recklessly after weeks of recovery that did it. She started falling back to earth and wasn't sure whether she would be able to recover fast enough to right herself. Luckily, Naren was able to do the catching, and gently swung her out of the air and descended back to the ground.

CHAPTER TWO

"We've got to leave now!" Naren yelled to Edgar and Symon as he landed and set Sera down. She was shaky, but able to stand on her own. Symon and Edgar were walking onto the field from a tunnel in the southeast corner of the stadium. Both of them had their hands wrapped around the grips of their elcycles, powerful electric motorcycles powered by their LO-EC energy. Walking with them was Eric, the person who had taken up the role of leading the rebellion in Pittsburgh.

"You're leaving!? After what just happened!?" Eric screamed.

"That happened because we're here!" Symon snapped back. "We need to get out of this city, and do it loudly enough that everyone knows we're gone."

"Sera told me the plan before she took off. Together we programmed the coordinates for her garden in New Orleans," Edgar said.

"We aren't going to New Orleans," Naren replied. Sera's head snapped up to look at him, then as she realized the issue, her head sank.

"Isn't it the closest place that we have a safe hideout?" Edgar asked.

"They just tried to bomb us here. If we get spotted entering New Orleans, the same thing will happen. It'd be the same no matter where we go. If there are peacekeepers there, then it isn't safe now."

"So where do we go?" Sera asked, her eyes filled with tears.

"Why are you all standing around?! We have to get to Symon's hideout!" Nadine screamed as she and Victor set their feet on the ground. She was happy and relieved to know she could now carry him with little effort. The last time she had tried, it was almost a disaster.

The plan clicked into place in everyone's head. They had spent weeks at Symon's hideout, an old house in an abandoned city called San Diego. It was now their best chance at hiding out without risking the lives of others.

"Eric, we're going to blast right through the peacekeeper's front line, make sure they know we've left the city. Go up into the lookout and signal to us if you see any targets we can hit," Naren directed.

"Victor, you'll be at the front. When we get the signal from Eric up high, you mow the road," Naren said. Victor nodded.

"Edgar, you'll be on an elcycle in the middle, with Sera riding in front of you," Naren continued. "If anyone gets close, you know what to do. Symon, you'll be in the back providing suppressive fire to our rear as we escape. Nadine and I will be up high and go wherever we're needed."

When Naren concluded his directions, everyone moved with haste. Edgar and Symon re-programmed the elcycles to go to San Diego and put them into position at the north of the field. Symon reached into one of the cargo bags on the elcycle and pulled out the retrofitted peacekeeper armor part that he'd had since the first major battle in Chicago. He slid his arm into the piece of armor and when it connected with the microtransformer in his hand, the mounted machine gun whirred to life, ready to fire once again. Naren helped Sera onto the other elcycle. Edgar hopped on behind her, and they were ready to go.

Their eyes all focused on the same spot, a broken window about halfway up the megaskyscraper nearest to the stadium. After about a minute, a hand poked out and started waving a long red cloth. That was the signal from Eric. It was time to go.

Victor sprinted off the field and through the tunnel that led outside. The rest of the team followed closely behind. From the way Eric waved, they knew peacekeepers were a few miles up the road, which made sense. By now, the LO-ECs knew the general pattern to how the peacekeepers moved. If they attacked from the south, like they had today, there was probably a larger staging area set up a few miles west, at the nearest bridge that still stood. The LO-ECs had attacked these staging areas a few times over the past few days. Now, as they approached, they prepared to do the same, but with one key difference; this time they weren't heading back to Pittsburgh afterwards.

Victor was so fast that by the time the peacekeepers could react to his appearance on the highway, he was already well within range to blast them with shock waves. Over and over, Victor threw his arms up from his side, and waves of air rushed forward and sent soldiers flying. There was no answer, no possible way for the soldiers to fight back. His speed and power were overwhelming. A few soldiers were able to quickly get back on their feet, but they met a different end shortly after, either from Naren and Nadine's dive bombs or Edgar's blades. Symon brought up the rear as instructed but scarcely needed to use his machine gun. Symon could have killed plenty of wounded, and even some soldiers who simply needed to get back to their feet, , but that wasn't the point today. They needed peacekeepers to survive and spread the word that the LO-ECs had left.

After hours of travel, the group felt confident that they weren't being followed. They stopped to eat and rest.

"Symon, do you know what this is?" Nadine asked as she tossed a small, dark grey cylinder to Symon. Symon started looking it over.

"A soldier was standing on a hill outside of the stadium and was using it to direct the missiles. It creates a really bright green light," Nadine continued.

Symon found a tiny trigger near one end of the cylinder and pressed it. Sure enough, as soon as the trigger was depressed, a bright green dot of light appeared on the ground.

"Turn it off!" Edgar yelled. "You'll let them know where to send the missiles!"

"No, that's not how this works," Symon replied, but complied with Edgar's request regardless.

"It almost looks like the light from a laser cannon," Sera said.

"I think that's what it is, just not nearly as powerful. You could probably make some sort of sensor for a missile to see this and aim for it, but there's no way it could sense the light from far away," Symon said.

"Okay, but that means…" Naren stopped as he pieced his thoughts together. "That means wherever the missiles were launched from, they didn't need precise coordinates. They just needed to send the missiles to the general Pittsburgh area, and then when they got near enough, the missiles followed the laser cannon light thing."

"But how did the soldier know to stand there?" Victor asked. "The missiles were slow for us, but there's no way a normal soldier could make it from their camp to that hill by the time they saw the missiles."

"They probably planned this for weeks," Nadine replied. "They attacked from the south today as a distraction to let their one soldier in the north get near the hill. Hell, all the attacks from the south over the past few weeks could have been an effort to focus our attention there. Once he was near the hill, all he had to do was wait until he saw the missiles appear over the horizon, and then those old-ass ion-thruster missiles were slow enough that he could point the laser light with time to spare."

"Damnit, I can't believe they caught us this off guard," Edgar said.

"When we hit Chicago, it must have been too much of a shock to them, they had no idea how to react," Sera said. "Now that we gave them time to slow down and plan things, they've caught up with us."

"So now we disappear, back to Symon's hideout, and figure out a way to shock them again," Nadine said. Everyone nodded.

CHAPTER THREE

"Oh, those fucking assholes!" Symon screamed.

"Stop fucking yelling!" Nadine yelled in reply.

"Both of you, shut the fuck up," Naren whispered sharply.

After a night of uneasy rest in the middle of nowhere, the six LO-ECs had been traveling since dawn along the old highways. Near the end of the journey, the road took them over low mountains that looked down into San Diego. But when they looked for the city, what had been abandoned buildings were now rubble and ash. The entire city was gone. The only recognizable pieces of humanity left were a few dozen military vehicles roaming the wasteland.

"They bombed the whole city?" Edgar asked, still in utter disbelief at the scene below them.

"I get it," Sera said. "They didn't want us to have a hideout to return to, keep us on the run," Sera said.

"How did they figure out this was our hideout? They found Symon's old house?" Victor asked.

"It's possible, but they could have also just bombed all the abandoned cities they could think of, knowing we must have hidden in one of them," Naren said.

"But they could have done that at any time while we were hiding out here, why did they wait till after we left?" Edgar asked.

"Spidre wanted us alive," Nadine said. "Remember after the fighting tournament in LA? They captured me alive and were transporting me to Spidre's compound. Same with Sera and the androids. We still have no idea why he did that, but bombing abandoned cities back then would have risked killing us."

Everyone stood silent for a moment.

"We have to move, the longer we stay the more chance we get spotted," Naren said.

"Where do we go?" Sera asked, very clearly exhausted.

"Just away from here for now, we can talk more long term later," Naren said.

Everyone turned to leave except Symon, who remained standing and facing the city, both fists clenched and vibrating with anger.

"Symon!" Naren whisper-shouted. Symon didn't move. Frustrated, Nadine swung herself in front of Symon and pushed him backwards. It wasn't a hard push, but it surprised Symon so much that he fell backwards.

"Sorry, but we have to move," Nadine said.

"I'm sorry. I just…" Symon said before stopping to gather himself. "That was my home for so long."

"I know. I know," Nadine replied. She reached down to help Symon up, but then suddenly her eyebrows raised, and she instead turned away from Symon and towards the bombed-out city.

"What the fuck are you doing!?" Naren said.

"What color are the vehicles at Symon's compound?" Nadine asked.

"What?!" Naren asked.

"When they captured me in LA, and were bringing me to

Spidre's compound, Spidre had a black elcycle. Are all the vehicles at his compound black?" Nadine asked.

"Why are we talking about this now?!" Sera exclaimed.

"Just answer the question!" Nadine shouted.

"Yes, the vehicles and uniforms at the compound are black. Who cares!?" Naren yelled in reply. Victor and Edgar threw their hands in the air.

Nadine stared down at the city for another few seconds.

"Can you tell from here if those vehicles are black?" Nadine asked. After another moment Naren understood, and stood shoulder to shoulder with Nadine, trying to get a better view.

"They might be, it's hard to tell," Naren said after some time.

"Oh, for fuck's sake," Victor said and was immediately a blur down the side of the mountain. Symon finally got up and dusted himself off, and they all watched as Victor weaved through the city towards a truck, and then returned up the mountainside.

"Yes, the vehicles and the uniforms are black. Can we get the fuck out of here now?" he asked.

Nadine and Naren nodded at each other. They had the beginnings of a plan, but discussing it would have to wait. They got back on the road again, going back the way they came for as long as they could. Finally, Symon signaled that he was going to stop.

"Fuck, how are we this exhausted?" Edgar said

"I imagine it's more of a mental thing than a physical. We've pushed harder than this before, but never with setback after setback like now," Nadine replied.

"It's not mental for all of us," Sera said through short breaths.

"If we're stopped, we should figure out where we're going next," Naren said. "I really only see two options, Chicago or New Orleans."

"Which is closer?" Victor asked.

"New Orleans, but not by much," Symon replied.

"Neither one is a great option," Nadine said. "If the peacekeepers spot us, we'll have to leave immediately, otherwise they'll bomb the city. Chicago's advantage is that there is a large area controlled by people we're friendly with, and all the soldiers are congregated in a few places, so they might be easier to avoid. New Orleans is closer, and from Sera and Naren's description, the garden that Sera's followers have will be a more comfortable place to rest. But the city is military controlled. We might be able to waltz right in undetected, or we get unlucky and a random patrol sees us and blows our cover. There is no way to predict it."

Everyone stayed quiet for a while. Finally, Sera broke the silence.

"I know I'm biased here, but I honestly think New Orleans is the better option," she said. "If one random soldier sees us, there is a chance we can kill him and hide the body. If we get spotted in Chicago, it'll be because we stumbled across a whole regiment."

"OK. Let's go to New Orleans," Naren said. He walked over to one elcycle and started programming it, while Nadine and Sera worked together to program the other. They were nearly done when Edgar finally spoke up.

"Sera, I'm sorry," he said, immediately drawing everyone's attention.

"What? For what?" Sera replied.

"I know somewhere we can go that is a better choice than New Orleans," Edgar replied.

Everyone was stunned. Edgar had rarely, if ever, spoken with such certainty.

"W-where?" Naren finally asked.

"Here, in this desert," Edgar responded, looking around the barren rocky terrain that surrounded them.

"We are not camping out in the middle of nowhere for weeks," Naren said. "Sera needs to recover, and we need food…"

"Not *here* here!" Edgar interrupted. "There is a settlement in this desert. It's to the north, and possibly a little east."

Nadine then remembered the stories Edgar told in the days after they first met.

"You're talking about the people who you lived with after you had to leave your aunt and uncle?" she asked. Edgar nodded in reply.

"There aren't any peacekeeper regiments watching over them?" Symon asked.

"There weren't when I last saw them. But that was a while ago," Edgar said.

"And they didn't care that you were a LO-EC?" Sera asked.

"I never told them, and they never asked," Edgar replied. "I figured the less they knew about me, the better for both of us if peacekeepers ever came. But they probably figured it out even though I didn't tell them. There's not a lot of reasons why a person would constantly wear fingerless gloves." As he said this, Edgar held up his hand, showing off the silver-grey circle embedded between his fingers that he had hidden for so long.

"They knew what was happening in the rest of the world?" Naren asked.

"Yes," Edgar replied.

"How?" Naren followed up.

"Some of their people had proper documents and worked on the transcontinental transit with my aunt and uncle," Edgar said. "TCT workers work on weeks-long shifts, so when their shift was over, they'd go back to their settlement with info, money, and any supplies that the settlement needed."

"Doesn't that mean they probably know we're being hunted by

literally the entire world army?" Victor asked.

"Probably," Edgar replied. Victor squinted at him.

"I never said we'd be guaranteed to stay," Edgar said. "I just said it was a better choice than New Orleans. If they don't want us to stay, we won't. But getting turned away peacefully today is better than getting turned away by force tomorrow."

Everyone stayed silent, as they gently nodded in agreement.

"Edgar, help me program the coordinates in the elcycle," Symon finally said.

CHAPTER FOUR

I wonder if they'll be surprised to see me, Edgar thought to himself. *Maybe they think I'm dead? No, wait, what the hell am I thinking? They must have heard about what was going on, right? And they would assume I'm involved somehow.*

Edgar was on foot, trudging through the desert by himself. He had left the group a couple miles back, with everyone in agreement that he should make contact first and then come back with the news, be it good or bad.

But if they figure I'm involved with the rebellion, isn't that even more reason for them not to let us stay? It was dangerous for them when it was just the Vegas battalion after me. Now the whole world's army wants me dead.

He was about to enter the village. Compared with the cities Edgar and the other LO-ECs usually resided in, this village was simple. Just several rows of single-floor buildings that were kept in remarkable shape given their age. The village was old, but it still looked alive despite there being no people outside at the moment.

On the other hand, I guess that was the case from the get-go, Edgar thought to himself. *The whole world's army wanted me dead back then, too. I just didn't know why, and the army didn't know I existed. Now, they know*

I exist but just don't know where I am. I guess that's almost the same thing.

More roads came into view. More older, well-kept houses, but still no people.

I wonder if they will even recognize me, though?" he thought as he looked down at his arms.

I'm so much bigger than I used to be, so much meatier. And my clothes are completely different. He was wearing a yellow hoodie and dark jeans that the locals in Pittsburgh had given him.

I wonder if my adopted family are all still living together?" Andrew had *been talking about moving out the last time I was here. He could have definitely gone out on his own by now. Jeana is probably still at home.*

By this time, Edgar had made his way to what he remembered as the center of town.

What can I say to convince them to let us stay? Should I tell them we're on the run? Or maybe that we're injured? I mean, I guess technically both of those things are true, right?

Despite his now-central location, Edgar still had not seen another person, but he was too lost in his own thoughts to notice.

No. No bending the truth, Edgar thought. *I tell them we attacked the net tower, got ourselves too injured to keep moving, compromised the safety of an entire city, and now need to lay low while a woman who can literally blow up the town recovers from injury so that we can make our next move to overthrow the government. That way if they decide to get involved in this, it'll be completely by their choice.*

Finally, Edgar looked around and saw that the street was lifeless despite all the buildings looking well kept.

"Where the hell is everyone?" Edgar said aloud. He slowed down his pace a little and started to look around more.

This doesn't make sense, Edgar thought. *If the whole village moved to a new location, why do all the buildings still look lived in?*

Edgar eventually found his way to the house of his old host family. As he approached and raised his hand to knock, the door swung open and there stood a 50-ish woman who was nearly the same height as Edgar. Edgar recognized her immediately but didn't get a chance to speak before she did.

"Get inside now!" the woman sharply whispered. Edgar complied and the woman glided the door shut behind him.

"Uhh, hi, Rose," Edgar blurted out as the side of his mouth curled into a little sheepish smile.

"Edgar!" the woman exclaimed and ran to give Edgar a hug.

A few seconds later, a girl about 11-years-old appeared in the doorway to the next room.

"Jeana!" Edgar exclaimed with a smile. The girl ran to join the hug.

"I've missed you two so much!" Edgar said as tears welled up in his eyes.

"I'm surprised you had time to miss us, you've been busy," Jeana said.

"Jeana! That's not appropriate!" Aunt Rose whispered again. "Now go get your father and your brother."

Their home was significantly larger than the modern megaskyscraper apartments. It comprised three rooms and had older, larger, but still all-electric, cooking equipment. The main room was fairly bare except for the cooking equipment, cushions to sit on and two bed rolls tucked away in the corner. Jeana went to each room and motioned for the people inside to come out. A short, chubby, older man came out of the room on the left, while a young man even taller than Edgar and Rose came out of the right.

"Dave! Andrew!" Edgar exclaimed.

"Shhh" Aunt Rose snapped, putting her index finger to her pursed mouth. Andrew and Dave came over and gave Edgar a long, silent hug.

"Still living here, eh?" Edgar quipped at Andrew as they finished.

"It's complicated" Andrew replied.

"Most things are complicated now," Dave said. Rose gave him a look.

"All we know is what we've heard," Rose said as she turned back to Edgar. Come. Sit. We want to know everything from your perspective."

As he moved to sit, Edgar thought about what to say. "Well, I guess I should start by saying that I know what I am now. If you want me to leave that out so that the kids don't know…"

"We told them," Dave said. "With everything that was going on, they started asking more and more questions. We finally had to come out with the truth."

"Okay, that makes this easier." Edgar took a deep breath.

"My Aunt and Uncle heard through the TCT about a fighting tournament with a huge payout in Los Angeles and thought it could be a way for me to live independently for a while, maybe forever. At the tournament another LO-EC was there and kicked the shit out of me. I foolishly used my powers to try and beat her and she used hers in turn. She got caught, and I helped her escape with the help of another LO-EC who was watching the tournament. We went to New Orleans to help her brother help his girlfriend, also both LO-ECs, destroy the androids that controlled the city. The brother and the girlfriend, I mean. The androids were just androids. And then another LO-EC revealed himself during our fight with the androids, so that's six of us in total. After that we planned, and trained, and attacked the army controlling Chicago. When that worked, we attacked Halifax and Gibraltar. When that worked, we attacked Monaco. That didn't work because Spidre called out the reserve troops from New York. So, we attacked the net tower in New York and brought it down, but severely injured ourselves in doing so. We stayed in Pittsburgh while recovering. Spidre launched a missile strike in Pittsburgh to try and end us while we were still injured. We were almost completely recovered at that point, though, and mostly stopped the missiles from doing damage, but the most powerful of us reinjured herself. We want to stay here while she recovers, after which I assume we'll attack Spidre and his compound and kill him once and for all."

Edgar paused for a moment to think if there was anything he'd missed.

"Oh, also, the woman that beat me up at the tournament is my romantic partner now, and the one who is injured has the ability to literally blow up a building. Oh, and Spidre is also a LO-EC. He can make blades out of energy come from his hands, which is the same power I have, but he can shoot his off like a laser beam. I can't do that."

Everyone stayed silent for a few seconds.

"Ah," Andrew said. "Dad's right. Everything is more complicated."

CHAPTER FIVE

"My ears and neck feel weird," Naren blurted out to the group. They had been waiting for Edgar to return for several hours now, with no sign of progress. Sera was sleeping in Naren's lap on the ground while everyone else sat on the rocky terrain.

"Let me see," Symon said as he got up and everyone else looked over at Naren.

"Oh, you're getting a sunburn," Symon said immediately.

"Sunburn?!" Naren exclaimed.

"That's a thing?!" Victor also exclaimed as his eyes darted around the sky. Everyone else was checking their own skin to see if it was different.

"You'll be fine, Victor, you spent 20 years outside," Symon replied. "Sera will be ok, too. The rest of us haven't experienced desert sun for this long before..."

"Wait, why will Sera be fine?" Nadine asked.

"Because she has more melanin," Symon replied. Everyone looked confused.

"What is melanin?" Victor asked.

"How do you know that?" Nadine asked the same time as Victor.

"Melanin is a pigment in your skin, Victor. It protects your skin from the sun. Sera has darker skin than us because she has more melanin, so she can stay out in the sun longer," Symon said.

Naren sighed. "Even now, she finds some way to be more powerful than us."

Everyone chuckled as Symon grabbed an extra shirt and gave it to Naren to cover his ears and neck.

"Do you think they'll let us stay?" Naren asked.

"Yes," Nadine replied simply. Everyone was taken aback by her assuredness.

"What? He would've been back already if they had said no," Nadine continued. "They must have heard about our battles and assumed Edgar might come back at some point. They would have had to make a firm decision. Either they would turn him and us away immediately, not get involved at all, or they would decide to help us, and have some sort of plan for doing so. The former would have ended quickly, the latter would have taken some time to explain, and been accompanied by all sorts of tearful reunions and stories."

Everyone was silent for a few moments.

"Well, you're rarely wrong about these things," Naren said. "Let's hope your streak stays alive."

A few minutes later, Edgar popped back into view. As he got closer, they could see he had a smile on his face.

"Sera, Edgar's back. We'll have to get moving soon," Naren said as he gently shook Sera awake.

"Why do you have a shirt on your head?" she asked Naren as she slowly got up.

"I got burned by the sun," Naren replied.

"That's a thing?!" Sera asked, but no one had a chance to answer as Edgar had come close enough to talk.

"It went well?" Symon asked.

"Oh, yeah. It went very well," Edgar beamed. "Cover up the elcycles."

"They're letting us stay with them?" Victor asked.

"Not exactly" Edgar replied. "I'll explain on the way. They said peacekeepers have been poking around more often lately. They're usually easily tracked, but you never know."

They quickly unpacked everything they needed from the elcycles and covered them with Symon's sand-colored tarps. Naren carried Sera on his back while everyone else carried the supplies.

"So, what's the story?" Symon asked Edgar as they started walking towards town.

"Well, basically, they had heard about all the LO-EC-led rebellions and figured I was involved. They also figured that at some point, there might come a time when we needed their help. So, they have spent all this time, basically since we attacked Chicago, preparing for our arrival."

Nadine smirked.

"Nadine already told you all of this, didn't she?" Edgar asked, noticing her expression.

"Of course," Naren replied.

"But this plan doesn't involve us staying with them?" Nadine asked.

"Not exactly" Edgar replied. "Let me start from the beginning. When we attacked Chicago, they heard about it. In fact, for a few days, it was all anyone talked about. They couldn't escape it. Everyone at the TCT station was having the same conversation about one thing: us. Just constant, hushed talk about how the city of Chicago, led by a bunch of LO-ECs, was able to take on the world's army and win."

Everyone started feeling bashful at the thought of being the topic of conversation for the entire world.

"They thought I might be involved in the fight in some way. So, they figured there was a chance I'd come back one day asking for help. And the whole town, and especially my host family, talked about it a lot. Eventually, they all came to the conclusion that if we ever came for help, they would provide it, but they would stick to the plan they thought up."

"And that plan is?" Symon asked with obvious anticipation. Edgar stayed silent for one extra moment.

"They built an entire town for us," he said. His voice cracked as he uttered the words, and his eyes welled up with grateful tears.

"A town?!" Sera exclaimed.

"That… why?" Symon asked.

"Well, really, they built a new town for themselves, then kept their old town in good shape for us to use," Edgar replied. "That way they could help us but also keep themselves hidden."

"I don't understand," Victor said.

"I… think I get it," Nadine finally piped up. "They thought Edgar might come back to the town he knew, and might be bringing at least five others, but didn't know if peacekeepers were going to be following him in. They couldn't risk their hidden society being attacked by Spidre's entire world army, so they knew they couldn't stay at the town Edgar knew. But they did want to provide what help they could and be nearby if needed. The only way to do that was to keep the old town in good shape. If they hadn't, when Edgar got there and saw it was abandoned, he would have either moved on to a new plan or tried to find their new town. Now we'll be close enough to help, but far enough that we're less likely to risk their survival."

"That's almost all of it," Edgar said. "The only people there when I arrived were my old host family. They've left now, but one of them will come every day to check if we need anything. They showed me where the daily-production crops were growing and showed me all the houses that have hiding spots in case the army comes. They asked that if that ever happens, that we hide first and fight only if it's the only option. The faster the army moves on, the better."

Victor tensed. The thought of hiding in a tiny space made his heart pound.

"That makes sense," Naren said. "Edgar, your host family are geniuses."

"Yeah, this is incredible," Sera agreed.

After a few more minutes of walking, the group made it to the house where Edgar had found his host family. He quickly showed them the hiding place, a tunnel to another house that was hidden under floorboards, and then finally, they lay down on the bed mats to rest.

CHAPTER SIX

Victor was the first to act. His movements a blur, he rushed forward and threw a jab. Nadine's instincts were still razor-sharp despite having been out of action for so long. She faded to the right and threw a punch with her left. Victor was too fast; his hand was already in front of his face waiting to block the blow. With each passing moment, the blows became faster and fiercer, yet both fighters refused to let a punch get through. Meanwhile, the eyes of everyone around were transfixed on the spectacle in front of them. Edgar, Sera, and Naren circled around to Symon, never once glancing away from the action.

"One day's rest and they're back at sparring," Sera said to Symon, while both of them still stared at the fight.

"You will join them soon enough, I promise," Symon responded. "No nausea when you ate?"

"A little, but it was gone in like two minutes," she replied.

Symon nodded. "Your body definitely seems like it's healing, and no setbacks from what happened a few days ago. If it makes you feel any better, had this all happened twenty years ago, your recovery might have been an award-winning research paper," he said with a chuckle. The comment helped. Sera laughed.

Suddenly, Victor dropped his hands and rushed forward. Nadine threw a punch that connected, but it did nothing to slow Victor down. His right shoulder buried itself in Nadine's chest and sent her tumbling to the ground. The laughter stopped. Every noise seemed to stop. Victor had finally landed a blow.

Nadine immediately popped up into a seated position to let everyone know she was ok. Victor joined her in sitting. He couldn't even celebrate his accomplishment, he was so exhausted.

"Holy shit!" Sera shouted. "That move was insane!"

"It… was," Nadine said through exasperated breaths.

"I've wanted… to try that one… for a while…" Victor replied. "Too bad… it'll only work once."

Nadine nodded. He was right, She wouldn't fall for that trick the next time they sparred. And the next time they sparred, she would not be as out of practice. Still, she knew this was a turning point. Victor was adapting, he was learning how to trick his opponent. And in terms of hand-to-hand combat, Nadine was among the most difficult to trick in the world.

"Naren, get these two some food please," Symon said. Naren nodded and flew off.

"Are you in any pain?" Symon said loudly to Nadine as he walked over to Victor.

"Just… my pride," Nadine replied as she remained seated.

"Ah. That'll have to recover on its own unfortunately," Symon said with a smirk.

"Sit up and hold out your arms please," Symon asked of Victor. Victor did as instructed. His arms were shaking, as they always did, but not particularly fast or violently.

"Make your wrists go limp," Symon further instructed. He

wanted to make sure Victor wasn't forcing his arms to stay more rigid. He wasn't.

"Ok. You're good," Symon said. "That's it for today, though. Unless some emergency defensive action needs your attention, you rest."

"Ok, ok, I will. Christ," Victor replied.

"There are some people walking towards the town," Naren said as he landed and started dispersing food. Everyone's heads perked up and looked around, quickly settling on the three figures coming from the north.

"It's my old host family," Edgar said. "Well, some of them."

"Uhh, hi everyone," Andrew said as he came within earshot.

"We're here to check in and see if there is anything you need," Rose said.

"I could use some basic medical equipment to check someone's vitals," Symon responded immediately. "Also, do you have anything that would relieve nausea?"

"I think so. Who is nauseous?" Dave asked.

"Me," Sera said. "I kind of fried my insides during the fight in New York."

"Whoa," Andrew replied. "I… don't think we have any medicine for that."

"I don't think anyone does, but the nausea meds are enough," Sera said.

"They will have to be," Rose said. "Do you need anything else?"

After a few moments of contemplative silence, Victor spoke up.

"Do you have any treatment that can fix being scared of small places?" he asked. Everyone's heads snapped to face him.

"Uhh. Small places?" Dave asked.

"Yeah, like small rooms," Victor said.

"I'm not sure I know what you mean," Rose replied.

"Yeah, I'm not sure I do either," Naren said.

"It's kind of hard to explain it," Victor said. "If I'm in a small room I get dizzy, my heart starts pounding, and I have to shut my eyes."

"Did this start after you got injured in New York? Or after you collapsed in Monaco?" Nadine asked.

"No, it's way older than that. At least since we all met each other," Victor replied.

"But not before that?" Edgar asked.

"I don't know," Victor said. "Before we met, I never really had to be in a small room. I was outside the whole time."

"So, what rooms have you been scared of?" Symon asked.

"Well…" Victor trailed off as he thought for a moment. "Even though I wasn't in it, the first time I remember the feeling was when I heard the story of Sera being in that special prisoner transport. When you tricked the androids into thinking they caught you and they put you in that big heavy oval thing."

"Ok. Were there other times?" Symon asked.

"There were other times like that, when the thought of a small area made me nervous," Victor said. "But for actually being in a small space, I can only think of two. When I took the ICT to Gibraltar and had to be in that little train car with no way to escape, and then the worst was in an elevator that time I went to Chicago to check it out before our assault."

"Why didn't you tell us before now?" Sera asked.

Victor shrugged. "I didn't think it was a big deal," he replied. "But those hiding places Edgar showed us are…" Victor stopped with a shiver.

"Ahhh, now it all makes sense. You're worried about it now because we need to hide rather than fight if soldiers come," Sera said. Victor nodded in reply.

"Well, when it comes to your stay here, the hiding places are just a last-ditch precaution," Andrew said. "We usually see the peacekeepers coming from miles out, and I'd imagine with three people who can fly you can see even farther. And even if we somehow miss them, the chances of them searching every single house are small. Eventually, they get tired of kicking in doors and they move on."

"Yeah, it's not likely your fear will ever have to be tested here," Rose said. "But there is no telling what will happen in the next phase of your plan, whatever it may be. Maybe your fear helps you, maybe it hurts you, maybe it doesn't do anything. But you all need to keep it mind now that you're aware of it."

Everyone nodded in agreement.

CHAPTER SEVEN

Sera's heart was practically beating out of her chest. After months of rest, recovery, and slowly gaining back strength, the time had finally come; she and Nadine were going to go all out in a sparring session. It was an especially momentous occasion because while they had fought in practice before, it was always on the ground, where Nadine had a clear advantage. Now that Nadine had mastered flying and Sera had fully recovered, their bout could finally enter three-dimensional space. Sera didn't have much of a strategy; she'd learned long ago that trying to plan for a fight with Nadine was impossible. All Sera could do was rehearse everything she knew in her head over and over, and hope it came back to her when the time was right.

You're smaller and faster, staying inside and keeping the pressure on is key, Sera thought to herself. *Doesn't matter if we're in the air or on the ground, if Nadine gets distance it becomes her fight. If you can get the fight to the air, things get easier, but you'll still have to land plenty of blows before she tires, whereas she only has to land one blow with her LO-EC power behind it to take you down.*

Nadine was crackling with excitement too. This was her

first hand-to-hand sparring match where it was unclear to her if she would win. Without his airbursts, Victor could still only occasionally land a hit despite his huge speed advantage. Edgar and Naren couldn't manage to do that even if they used their powers, and Symon rarely participated in sparring, knowing everyone else was on a completely different level. On the ground, she was still confident in her ability to take Sera on, but Sera could take off on a dime and immediately turn the battle into an aerial dance where it was anyone's game.

Out of an abundance of caution, and to avoid making their host family nervous about too much noise, the group of six LO-ECs had traveled a few miles into the desert and out of the town they were currently calling home. They had done this any time a particularly loud or lengthy practice was needed, and so far, it had been successful. The month had gone by quietly, and now one last sparring match stood between them and the next phase of their plan.

Sera and Nadine finished warming up and turned to face each other. The tension was so high the others in the group were holding their breaths in anticipation. Symon stepped forward to call the start of the fight, and even he was nervous, not wanting to mess up his call and give one fighter or the other an accidental advantage. He looked at Sera, who was about 15 feet to his left, then at Nadine, who was an equal distance away to his right, then looked straight ahead of him.

"Begin!" he yelled and immediately backed away to the rest of the group.

Sera and Nadine reacted at practically the same time. Sera took to the air, but Nadine saw this coming and took off to intercept. Nadine grabbed Sera around the hip and threw her back towards the ground. Sera touched down to the ground relatively gently, but

Nadine stayed right on her and knocked Sera to the ground with a diving tackle. Sera landed on her back and Nadine landed on top of her. Nadine maneuvered to straddle Sera and cocked her fist back. Nadine's punches started raining down and it took all of Sera's focus to get her head out of the way in time. Nadine only managed to get glancing blows, but even those stung like crazy.

Finally, Sera darted a hand up between Nadine's arms and grabbed a wrist as it coiled back to begin another strike. Sera managed to grab Nadine's other wrist as well, and they struggled against each other, alternating between pulling away and pushing together, each hoping to somehow gain an advantage. Finally, Sera moved Nadine off of her enough so that Sera could use her powers to swing out from under Nadine and drag her into the air. Nadine let go of Sera and activated her own powers, her hands and feet lighting up with the blue glow of energy that kept her aloft. As they both went airborne, the tide of the fight changed. It was Sera's turn to throw blows now. Her advantage in aerial speed and maneuverability showed as she danced around Nadine, throwing many blows and landing some. Nadine did her best to predict and was often successful, but without firm ground under her to anchor her moves, she was just that fraction of a second slower than usual.

As the fight wore on, it started to take its toll. Nadine was getting dizzy from all the landed blows, and Sera was getting exhausted from having to dish out so much after first defending herself from certain defeat. Nadine saw the exasperation on Sera's face and knew her one chance was coming. Sera came forward with a swing that was slightly too wide, and Nadine had her opening. The blue aura enveloped Nadine's hand as she threw a jab past Sera's swing. Sera saw her mistake and the blow coming at her but knew there was nothing she could do. Both Sera and Nadine's punches connected, and they fell out of the sky. They landed on their backs, motionless on the ground, staring up at the sky, taking in giant breaths.

A second or two passed. None of the spectators moved. Finally, Symon walked towards the fighters but stopped when he heard noise coming from Sera and Nadine. Another second and everyone in the group recognized the noises to be low chuckles coming from both fighters. The chuckles became louder and louder until they were full on giggling out of a mix of exhaustion and exhilaration. Smiles crept onto the faces of Naren, Edgar, Victor and Symon. It was official: Nadine and Sera were recovered and able to fight at full power without issue.

Nadine slowly made her way back to her feet and walked over to Sera as Sera did the same. When Sera was fully up, Nadine wrapped her arms around Sera with a big hug.

"You're back," Nadine said.

"I am!" Sera exclaimed.

Nadine and Sera ate some food and recovered while everyone else ran through a more typical round of workouts and sparring. Once that was finished, they all made their way back to the village. When they got back, Rose, Dave, and Andrew were at the house waiting for them.

"It went well?" Dave asked, knowing the importance of the day's events.

Sera nodded. "I'm at full strength. We are ready."

Dave nodded.

"Did you find a map?" Naren asked. Andrew nodded and held aloft a rolled-up laminated piece of paper.

"Excellent," Naren responded. "Let's go inside and discuss the plan one more time with the map in front of us."

Everyone went inside and gathered around in a circle. Naren

rolled out the map in the middle of everyone and put rocks on each corner to keep it from rolling back up.

"Okay, so this map is a little old," Symon said as soon as he looked at the paper. "Earth isn't this green anymore, but otherwise this is accurate. It is a map of the entire world."

"Perfect. This is much better than looking at the display on the elcycle," Naren said.

"Ok, here is San Francisco, where Spidre's compound is located," Symon said, placing a small rock on the eastern shore of the Pacific Ocean.

"So, this is our end goal," Naren said as he pointed at the rock. "Spidre and his inner core of government operate out of a huge compound here. As I've mentioned before, it's hard to know exactly how many soldiers are stationed here, but it could very well be the same amount as we faced in New York. But the soldiers here wear black uniforms, and we saw soldiers clad in black doing surveillance work in San Diego. That means that at least some of Spidre's troops are being reassigned elsewhere, away from the compound, so the best chance we will ever have to successfully attack is now. But as you all know, soldiers aren't the only thing protecting Spidre. He also has an impenetrable force field surrounding the whole compound, which receives its power from the five supermassive power plants around the world. They are in Nuuk, the capital of Greenland; Quito, in South America; Sapporo, on the Japanese island of Hokkaido; Brisbane, in Australia; and Praia, on the Cape Verde Islands near Africa."

As Naren listed these places off, Symon placed rocks at each location on the map.

"In order to take down the force field, we need to get the power either shut off or disconnected at all five of these plants. If we miss even one, there is a chance the field stays active and we can't get in," Naren continued. "We also need to hit all five plants at more or less the same time, so that Spidre does not get word of what we're doing, figure out our plan, and start the process of pulling more power from the big fusion reactor in Istanbul that powers the rest of the world."

Symon put another rock on the map to mark Istanbul.

"If he successfully re-routes power from Istanbul, it makes this plan infinitely more complicated," Nadine said.

"Correct," Symon said. "The fusion reactor is the most heavily protected location in the world, even more than Spidre's compound or the net tower in New York. If it gets blown up, it could destroy the planet, so it was well fortified even before Spidre seized power. And disconnecting it from the grid is more difficult because it is connected to the entire world. The five supermassive plants are only connected to Spidre's force field so it's essentially only one connection to sever."

"But the complexity of the fusion reactor works to our advantage if we succeed in disrupting the five supermassive plants," Sera said. "Between the routine needed to reroute power to the force field, and the communication delays we created by destroying the net tower, it would take a full day or two to get power back to Spidre's force field."

"So, we hit all five supermassive plants at once so Spidre doesn't get a chance to react to our plan, then rush in to attack during the day or two at most that the force field is down," Edgar said.

"Correct!" Naren exclaimed. "And then Sera disables the force-field generator with her blast, so that if we do have to retreat or regroup the force field won't come back on. After that, it's just a matter of methodically taking down the forces that meet us, finding Spidre, and ending him.”

Everyone stayed silent, staring down at the map.

“So, who is attacking which plant?” Rose finally asked.

“Oh, right, we never discussed that with you all,” Naren said. “Victor will attack the plant in Praia and then use his speed to run across the Atlantic Ocean and North America to get to San Francisco in time. I will make the far flight to Brisbane since I’m the fastest flyer. Nadine will go to Nuuk since she’s the slowest flyer and that’s the closest location. Sera will take Sapporo and fly from there. Edgar will go to Quito and use an elcycle at full speed to get to San Francisco in time. Symon will wait things out and then meet us in San Francisco when the time comes.”

“And when is that time?” Andrew asked.

“Six days from now,” Naren replied. “We leave tomorrow for our cities, have a day or two to rest up from the travel, and then the big show begins.”

“Is the spot where we’re meeting up before attacking on this map?” Victor asked.

“Technically yes, but it’ll be hard to see,” Symon replied. “Let’s go over to the elcycle to compare.”

They all walked over to the elcycle and Symon brought up the holographic projection of the nav system. He fiddled with the display a bit and it brought up an aerial view of San Francisco Bay, then used his arm to brace the paper map against his chest to hold it open.

“Ok, so here is San Francisco, this spot here,” Symon said pointing first at the hologram, then at the same spot on the map.

“And here is where we’re meeting up,” Symon said as he fiddled with the projection again so it slid over to display a small mountain to the east of San Francisco.

"We will want to meet on the east side of this mountain near the peak, so anyone coming from the west will need to make a wide berth to avoid being seen," Symon said.

Everyone nodded in acknowledgement.

"I remember at one point someone saying Spidre wanted to capture you all alive in the past, right?" Rose asked.

"Yes, and we never figured out why," Nadine said. "But at the start of all this I was caught by Byron, one of the most ruthless and powerful captains in the world army, and rather than kill me immediately, he put me on a prisoner transport to send me to Spidre. The androids in New Orleans did the same to Sera, and they were even more cold and uncaring than Byron. When Naren was still an investigator working with the androids, they even outright told him Spidre had given commands not to kill any LO-EC found alive."

"So there is still some unknown here, and if your plan succeeds, you will be on a collision course with that unknown. Aren't you at all concerned about that?"

"Very," Naren said. "And if, or when, that unknown reveals itself, I sincerely hope we're ready."

CHAPTER EIGHT

That night, everyone tried their best to rest, but little sleep came to anyone. All the fights and pain that they had endured was finally coming to its conclusion, and nerves were high. When morning came, they ate one final meal with their host family and prepared to leave.

"Nadine, were you planning on stopping in Halifax on your way north?" Victor asked. Months earlier, the two of them, along with Edgar and Symon, had successfully brought down the local military regiment that controlled Halifax. After, they'd helped the locals set up defenses to keep it free of Spidre's control.

"I was thinking about it," Nadine replied. "It's a good point to stop and rest, and I'd like to give our fellows some heads up about the plan we're about to undertake." Among the locals in Halifax was a small group of LO-ECs that, with a lot of planning and luck, had successfully remained alive and hidden from Spidre's army. Their power level was similar to Symon's; they were stronger and faster than normal humans and could power devices like the elcycle, but they were not overwhelming powerhouses like Nadine and Victor.

"I think I want to come with you, and take the ICT line to Europe," Victor said with a great amount of timidity in his voice.

Everyone's gaze turned to Victor. There was an InterContinental Transit line that connected Halifax and Gibraltar, and thanks to their actions a few months ago, both of those cities were free of Spidre's control. The transit line could be used to get back and forth across the Atlantic Ocean. And Gibraltar was much closer to Praia then any point on the west side of the Atlantic. However, because of Victor's claustrophobia and ability to run across water, everyone figured he would run to Praia rather than take the ICT.

"You sure you'll be ok?" Edgar asked.

"That's a bold step, Victor," Naren said at the same time.

"I don't know if I will be ok, but I did it once already. I know what to expect," Victor said. "And I need to save my energy for the craziness afterwards. Lying low and resting in Gibraltar is the right choice for our strategy, right?"

"If you feel you can handle that mentally, then yes," Nadine said.

"And of course you know what I have to say about it," Symon said with a smirk. Victor smiled back, but it was Symon's usual concerns that led him to this decision. No matter what Victor's personal fears were, the risk of collapsing like he had in Monaco had to be lessened as much as possible.

"You can do this," Sera said, looking Victor dead in his eyes. "Just close your eyes as soon as you get on the ICT. Keep them closed and keep breathing until you get to Gibraltar. You'll make it."

Victor nodded. After some more last-minute preparations, they said their final goodbyes to each other and to their host family.

"Give them hell in Nuuk," Edgar said to Nadine.

"Don't die in Quito," Nadine said back, and they smiled at each other before embracing for one last time. Naren and Sera were traveling the same direction for a time, so the six LO-ECs finally departed in four different directions, hoping to see one another again in San Francisco six days from now.

Nadine flew overhead while Victor sprinted across the arid landscape. They avoided major cities and only briefly stopped for breaks along their route. They agreed it was best to stop just outside of Halifax and assess whether the peacekeeper forces were light enough to sneak into the city without being detected. They arrived just as dawn was breaking, and it became obvious very quickly that sneaking into the city wasn't an option.

"This is a pretty big regiment," Nadine said as she landed next to Victor, having just completed some reconnaissance from high in the air. "They're well-armed, too. Tanks, mounted guns, and lots of peacekeepers. Halifax was pretty-well fortified when we left. They can probably hold them off, but I don't know how long it would take."

"Could we beat them?" Victor asked.

"Easily," Nadine responded. "But if we get involved, we'll have to kill every single soldier. If even one survives and gets word back to Spidre, our plan will be at risk."

Victor cracked his knuckles and stretched his neck.

"So, what's the plan?" he asked.

"I'll fly over and attack head on from the other direction. Hopefully some locals will see me and follow the charge. I'll focus on the heavy artillery and force them to retreat in your direction. And when they get close enough…"

"I finish them, got it," Victor said. Nadine nodded and took off high in the air. She flew over the peacekeeper forces and when she saw bullets flying in the direction she came from, she knew she must be over the local forces who were holding the peacekeepers back. She descended with all the speed she could muster. When she passed close to the locals, she made a hard turn back towards the peacekeepers. She kept her eyes open for anyone who had a radio in their hand, and when she saw one, she immediately headed in that direction. Before the peacekeepers could turn to fire on her, she had barreled through the first soldier and deep into the line.

She took off again and stayed just overhead of the soldiers. By the time any single soldier could take aim, she was already gone, too far past for them to have a clear shot amongst all the other soldiers around them. The machine guns mounted to vehicles had a better chance of aiming at her, but they were also too slow. Any volley of fire they opened on her just hit other peacekeepers as she raced by. One by one, she circled the mounted machine guns, closing the spiral tighter and tighter until she could come at them head on and rip the guns from their mounts.

The tanks required even less effort to bring down. They were so slow that she could simply come up on them from the side and when she got close enough, throw a kick down onto the barrel and dislodge it from its moorings. As she did this, the locals figured out what was happening and started pressing hard at the front line. The peacekeepers gave in to panic and turned to retreat, but the trap was set. Victor was there waiting, alternating between running to intercept groups of fleeing peacekeepers and throwing air bursts to completely level them. In about an hour, the peacekeeper forces had dwindled to a few hundred, who gave up and surrendered to local forces. As the fighting ceased, Nadine found Victor and they made their way through the local forces until Nadine saw the familiar face of a local LO-EC.

"Hi, have you met Victor?" Nadine said with a smile.

CHAPTER NINE

"Will! Over here!" Nadine yelled to the LO-EC she had introduced Victor to the previous night. Victor was about five feet away, helping some locals remount a machine gun that Nadine had torn off during the battle. The man who Nadine called to, Will, looked around for another second before his eyes settled on Nadine farther down the street. He jogged over to her.

"Did you find any more radios?" Nadine asked as Will came close.

"Yes, but they were being carried by soldiers who we shot before you came," Will replied. "It is unlikely anyone had a chance to use the radio to let someone else know you're here."

"Good. Still, we shouldn't stay long. We'll rest for a little while, maybe get a couple hours of sleep, then get out of here," Nadine said. Victor and Will nodded.

"Let me bring you both to my apartment and you can rest," Will said.

Nadine and Victor followed Will to the megaskyscraper complex a few blocks away. Nadine and Will took the elevator up to Will's apartment on the 17th floor while Victor sprinted up the stairs. They ate some food and even managed to sleep for an hour or two before it was time to depart. The rest wasn't nearly enough given all the traveling and unexpected fight, but it would have to do. Nadine walked Victor over to the ICT station, where a train was waiting. Victor's jaw and fists clenched as he approached it. Nadine noticed and grabbed his hand.

"You'll be ok, Victor. You can do this," Nadine said.

"I can, but I sure don't want to," Victor said.

"Look at it this way. After this is over, you won't ever have to deal with small spaces again. You will be free to find the biggest fucking field in the world and never leave it," Nadine said. Victor's mouth curled into a little smile.

"Thanks, Nadine," Victor replied and with one last big breath, turned to get on the train. Nadine turned away as well and took off to the north.

Nadine's flight north was uneventful, aside from it getting progressively colder as she flew. She had food and clothes wrapped up and tied to her back, but she didn't want to risk untying everything while flying and potentially losing vital supplies. By the time she made it to Nuuk, it was nighttime, and she was shivering uncontrollably. She went straight for the nearest mountainside to land and throw all of her layers on. It helped some, but the time to attack the powerplant and make the mad dash to San Francisco was still about a day and a half away. She would need to find better shelter till then.

She took to the air again and took another survey of the area. At the northern shore of a bay was one relatively small megaskyscraper complex, which was the only major light source visible for hundreds of miles. Next to that, she could make out one huge structure, a dome about half as tall as the megaskyscrapers and easily over a mile wide. She assumed that was the supermassive power plant. She flew downward, closer to the shoreline, and from that vantage point she was able to see multiple abandoned buildings across the landscape. She flew to one near the western shore, as far away from the megaskyscrapers as she could get, and went inside. Its interior matched the outside. It was an abandoned warehouse of some sort, and up in the corner was what looked like an old office that was fully enclosed. It would do for the brief time she had to stay.

She stayed in that office for an uneventful, boring two days until finally, it was time. As she left the warehouse and began flying, she realized that some of her team had probably already started assaulting their power plants. Some might have even already finished, or failed to take the plant down, but she would have no idea. It didn't matter. She had to do her part and hope everyone else did theirs.

As she approached the power plant, sirens started blaring. She had been spotted, but it was ok. She hadn't planned on going for a covert operation anyway. Snipers with laser cannons perched at various spots along the plant's black exterior opened fire but were only able to get a handful of shots off before she busted through an entrance near the base of the structure. As she crumpled the door and landed in the hallway, a flood of civilian employees who had been heading towards that same doorway stopped in their tracks.

"Turn around and leave this place now!" she screamed over the alarms. The employees stumbled over each other but turned to get away from Nadine as fast as possible. When a gap opened, she darted through it and continued deeper into the structure. She passed several other rooms and eventually found a stairway leading downward.

Several months prior to this day, the LO-ECs had had a fortunate stroke of luck: they ran into a woman named May who was sympathetic to their cause, a master electrical engineer, and unabashedly attracted to Symon. Nadine knew from information May provided that the best way for her to cut the power from this plant was to take out the transformers on the lower levels. The rest of the plant would be undamaged and the transformers could be replaced easily enough, but it would take a week or two for that to be completed. In the meantime, no power would come from this plant. It was the perfect window of time needed.

Nadine kicked down the door to the stairwell and in doing so, sent a peacekeeper on the other side of the doorway flying. She ran onto the stairway landing. To her left, down the stairs, were dozens of peacekeepers marching upward in a single-file line. Each soldier had an electric sword on their arm, the blade crackling and sparking from the power running through it. The closest soldier took a swing upward at Nadine but was hopelessly slow. Nadine ducked around it and threw a single palm thrust into the soldier's chest, sending them flying backwards into the others lined up farther down the stairwell. Nadine leapt over them towards the nearest peacekeeper who was still on her feet. As she landed, Nadine buried her shoulder into this new soldier's chest, and the soldier went flying into the concrete wall. Another soldier went for a swipe, and Nadine dodged and flipped him over the railing. Another ran forward, and this one was thrown violently into the same concrete wall as his fellow peacekeeper. By now, some soldiers Nadine had leapt over were getting back on their feet, but before they could find their balance, Nadine jumped into the air and then slammed back down on the landing with all her might.

The whole staircase shook and groaned, and bolts connecting the stairs to the walls cracked in half. The landing Nadine was on, and all the stairs two flights above and below, fell inward away from the wall. Some peacekeepers managed to hold on for dear life, but many toppled over and down to the bottom of the well. Nadine activated her powers and floated in the center of the stairwell as carnage ensued around her. When everything stopped moving, she descended past mangled stairs and screaming peacekeepers until the area around was clear.

She turned and descended by flying head-first down the remaining stairs, past more peacekeepers swinging at her in vain. When she made it to the bottom floor, she quickly threw all the nearby peacekeepers away from her, then crashed through the nearest door. In front of her was a surprisingly large, windowless, concrete room full of dozens of round metal objects that measured about thirty feet in diameter. These were the transformers. She ducked back into the stairwell and grabbed a peacekeeper who was still conscious and grasping at his injured leg.

"Is this the only transformer room?" she asked.

"Wh-what?" he replied.

"Is this the only room in this building with transformers in it!?" she bellowed.

"Y-Yes!" the peacekeeper stammered in reply. Nadine tossed him away from her and turned back towards the transformer room. She ran towards the nearest transformer and when she was within striking distance, she spun around and kicked it while activating the energy in her legs. The transformer's shell buckled and crashed inward, and the mechanisms inside whirred to a halt. She looked to the next transformer, but above it on an elevated walkway, she saw peacekeepers with machine guns attached to their armor filing out of another staircase and lining up to fire on her.

Nadine took to the air and started a wide circle towards them. As she got closer, it became more and more difficult for them to aim at her. She was below them and the elevated walkway they were standing on was getting in the way. They had all practically stopped firing by the time she made it to the walkway, grabbed a beam on the bottom of it, and ripped the entire platform away from the wall. She let go and the walkway and soldiers dropped to the floor below. The platform landed on another of the transformers and crushed it.

Nadine spent the next few minutes in that room, alternating between ripping transformers apart and dispatching any and all peacekeepers who dared to try and stop her. As she crushed another of what must have been dozens of transformers, the lights in the room dimmed and then completely went out. She had done it. The power was out.

She crushed several more transformers just to be safe and then flew as fast as the space around her would allow back to the stairwell she'd entered from, up it, and out of the building. As she flew away, the only sound was the wind in her ears and the occasional laser cannon shot passing overhead.

She had completed her part of the plan and had done it with relative ease. As she headed southwest towards San Francisco, she hoped her teammates were having just as much luck in their parts of the world.

CHAPTER TEN

Victor had been at this station once before, when they first attacked Halifax months ago. Back then, he'd had to first help Nadine, Symon, and Edgar take down the ICT's emergency shutdown station before jumping on the train to Gibraltar and helping Naren and Sera clear the peacekeepers out of that city. It had been a frantic scramble to get on the train and then a terrifying few moments of waiting for the doors to close as soldiers descended to the platform, with no way for Victor to escape and no way for him to defend himself without risk of damaging the train. Memories of that day were adding on to Victor's claustrophobia, and tears flooded his eyes as he stepped onto the train. Through his blurred vision, he could faintly make out the shape of a bench of seats in front of him, and he ran for it, curled his knees up to his face and wrapped his arms around his legs. He buried his face and did not move from that position. He assumed other people were on the train and assumed they were looking at him, but he did not care.

After what seemed like an eternity, an automated soothing voice came on over the train's loudspeaker.

"This train is commencing slowdown procedure for final arrival in

Gibraltar. Please gather your belongings and prepare to disembark."

"Oh, thank fucking Christ," Victor whispered to himself. He felt the train slow down, then stop, then he heard a gentle hiss as the doors of the train opened. When he felt the warm outside air hit his arms, he finally lifted his head anddashed off the train and onto the platform in Gibraltar. It was then that he noticed how heavily he was breathing, and he made a conscious effort to slow it down.

"Ok, hard part is over," he said to himself out loud.

"You must be Victor," Victor heard someone say to his right. At the same time, he heard what sounded like a weird bird chirp.

Victor turned to look and saw a man he did not recognize standing there . He stood about the same height as Victor but had broader shoulders. The man was wearing clothes that Victor didn't recognize either. He had on a white collared shirt and black pants and shoes, but then also a black jacket made of cloth over his shirt, and a single thin piece of black cloth hanging down from the middle of the collar. All of his clothes were perfectly, spotlessly, eerily clean.

"How the fuck do you know my name?" Victor asked.

"We know a lot about you. Things will be made clear once my employer's train arrives..."

"I don't know what an employer is, and I don't care to find out. Who the fuck are you and why do you know my name!?" Victor replied.

"Calm down! You are making a scene!" the man whisper-yelled, looking around at the few people still on the platform who were slow to get off the train. Victor grabbed the man under the chin and held him aloft, and in doing so caused the few people around to hasten their exit.

"You do not tell me what to do!" Victor snapped back. "Either you tell me who you are or you die, those are the options."

The man's eyes were filled with panic as they stared down at Victor.

"Victor, we have been expecting you," another voice said, but it was coming from the back pocket of the man's pants. Victor reached around and grabbed what he immediately recognized as a radio, like the one the soldier in Pittsburgh had.

"The person you are currently threatening works for me and is only doing as I instructed, please do not harm him," the voice on the other end of the radio said.

"Oh, what the fuck is this now!?" Victor yelled.

"I imagine this is confusing for someone like you, but rest assured you are not at risk of any harm," the voice said. "The radios we are talking through are on a secured channel, meaning no one besides us knows that we are talking or where you or I are. My subordinate in front of you has been awaiting your arrival and let me know when he found you."

That must have been the bird chirp I heard, Victor thought. *It must have been some feature this radio has to quickly give this other person a signal I was spotted.*

"My subordinate's purpose has been fulfilled, so he is no longer of use," the voice continued. "You may kill him if you wish, but if you leave before I arrive at that station, I will immediately let the nearest military installation know you have been spotted in Gibraltar."

Victor looked up at the terrified eyes staring down at him and understood. He wasn't sure how, or by whom, but he had fallen into a trap, and the person he was holding up in the air was not the one who had laid it. He let the man go.

"I will wait right in this spot," Victor said into the radio before crushing it.

"Did you even know I was a LO-EC?" Victor asked the man.

"W-What is a LO-EC?" the man answered as he staggered, trying to stand upright again.

"Ah, so you know absolutely nothing," Victor replied.

"I was j-just shown ph-photos of you and five other people and told to wait here and report if I saw one," the man replied.

"How long have you been here?" Victor asked.

"Three months," the man replied.

"Fucking Christ," Victor said. A thought then came to him.

"Are you the only one waiting, or are there others like you in other cities?" Victor asked.

"There is a whole team of us spread out in key locations all over Europe," the main said.

"Fucking Christ!" Victor said. He had difficulty imagining anyone could afford to pay so many people to essentially do nothing for that long.

"Who do you work for and how does he have that much money?" Victor asked.

"I have the pleasure and honor to serve Maximillion Bennington the Fourteenth!" the man replied. He said it with such pride that Victor almost felt bad letting him know he had never heard that name before and had no idea who Maximillion was.

"Mr. Bennington is the greatest of the world's remaining industrial tycoons!" the man continued. "His prowess and cunning in the business world are unmatched!"

"I have no idea what any of that means, but it sounds impressive," Victor replied. "And what is your name?"

"I'm Lenny," the man replied.

"Lenny, do have any idea why this Maximanial guy cares about me?" Victor asked.

"Maximillion. I do not. But you will be able to ask him yourself when he gets here. His personal train should arrive on that platform shortly," Lenny said while pointing at the TCT track and platform at the far corner of the station that Victor had never noticed before. It took a moment of studying it for him to realize it hadn't been there the last time he was here, and it looked like the entire platform had come up out of a hidden compartment in the ground. Victor could see that the TCT track led down into a tunnel, and he could only imagine where it led.

This guy has his own hidden platform!? What the fuck have I gotten myself into here!? Victor thought. The possibilities whirred around his head for another few minutes until he saw a short, golden-colored TCT train pull in to the platform.

CHAPTER ELEVEN

As the golden train made the typical hissing and whirring noises that accompanied a recent stop, a door near the rear slid open. On the other side of it stood a man about three inches shorter than Victor, wearing odd clothing similar to what Lenny was wearing, but this person's set had all sorts of odd lines and patterns stitched onto it. It was difficult for Victor to tell how old this person was. He first thought the man was Symon's age, but his skin was weirdly smooth and his hair unnaturally black and full. The man took a half step forward and looked around with his nose and mouth curled in an obvious look of disgust. However, his face softened somewhat when he made eye contact with Victor.

"It is a pleasure to finally meet you, Victor. I am sure you know who I am," the man said.

"Yeah, Lenny told me. You're Maximonious Paddington right?" Victor responded.

"Maximillion Bennington the Fourteenth," the man responded with a huff.

"Sorry. Hey what is that that you and Lenny are wearing?" Victor asked.

"What?" Maximillion replied.

"You're wearing a jacket even though it's hot as balls out and you have that extra cloth thingy hanging from your neck," Victor said.

"Oh, it is a suit and tie," Maximillion responded. "I'm sure the sort of folk you acquaint yourself with do not wear such fanciful appointments, but they are commonplace among us industrial elite."

"Yeah, I don't know what that is. I also don't know what you want with me," Victor said.

"Step onto my train and we can discuss it further," Maximillion replied.

"Yeah…That's not going to happen," Victor replied.

"Victor, I can understand your concern, but I assure you I have no intention of harming you. If I did, I would have let the military know you were here the second my subordinate spotted you," Maximillion responded, gesturing at Lenny while speaking.

"I…" Victor began to reply.

"Besides, my train is much nicer and more spacious than that dreadful ICT line, and much cleaner than this station," Maximillion continued while looking around with disgust in his face again.

Victor had heard the key word 'spacious' and conceded to poke his head into the car. Maximillion was right. Despite the train being significantly smaller than the ICT, it seemed much more roomy without the bench seating and the bulkheads separating everything. The interior was colored in all gold and red. At the far end of the car was a lady dressed the same way as Lenny was, and she was standing behind a golden-colored countertop with all sorts of bottles strapped to the wall behind her. To the left of the countertop, in the center of the far wall, was a door leading to another area of the train. Along the two longer walls were all different sizes and shapes of paintings. On the left wall was a short bench that had giant, red, fluffy, cushions lining it. The wall opposite that had a table that could fit five people at most, with a red tablecloth draped over it.

"Where is the train going to go?" Victor asked.

"Where do you want to go?" Maximillion asked in return.

"Praia," Victor replied without thinking.

"Ahh the power plant, that's your plan," Maximillion replied. "I happen to have a small mansion nearby. This train will take us right to it; it will take but an hour."

"Ok, sure." Victor replied. He was nervous, but the alternative of having his location revealed to the military and their plan potentially exposed seemed the worse of the two options at this point. He stepped onto the train, Maximillion followed, and Lenny embarked just behind them.

"Jenny, this is Victor, my personal guest. Serve him," Maximillion said to the woman behind the counter.

"Of course! What can I get for you, Victor?" Jenny asked.

"Oh uh. I don't think I need anything?" Victor responded.

"Surely you must be famished or parched from your journey?" Maximillion asked.

Victor thought for a moment.

"Do either of those words mean hungry? I could use something to eat," Victor eventually said.

"Yes, I heard you LO-ECs have quite an appetite," Maximillion said. "Fetch him something," Max said as he turned to Jenny.

"At once!" Jenny replied and disappeared through the door next to the counter.

"Please take a seat, let's chat you and I," Maximillion said.

As the train pulled out of the station, Victor plopped down on the cushioned bench and was astounded by how soft it was.

He had never felt anything like this in his life. He very nearly had to hold back tears from how overwhelmingly soft the bench felt. Maximillion sat down at the other end of the bench.

"So this train takes you wherever you want?" Victor asked.

"Not anywhere. My ancestors built this so we could quickly get to any place where we had major capital investments," Maximillion replied.

"Your ancestors? That is, all the Maximaniacs who were numbered one through thirteen?" Victor asked.

"You can just call me Max if it is so much trouble for you to say the full name," Maximillion said through gritted teeth.

"Max, got it," Victor replied.

"And you are correct. Over the course of generations, my ancestors acquired a great many assets that necessitated this train so that we may travel between them expeditiously," Max replied.

Victor stared blankly. Max sighed.

"I own a lot of stuff that my ancestors bought and sometimes need to get to them quickly," Max said.

"Oh. What do you own?" Victor asked.

"Many things. Near Gibraltar there is a factory that makes the cooking appliances that are in standard megaskyscraper apartments. I own that. More important to our conversation, though, I own the power plant in Praia."

"You own a whole power plant?!" Victor replied, but the conversation had to halt there as Jenny came back holding a huge tray of food. She placed it on the table and Victor couldn't even fully comprehend what he was looking at. All sorts of meats and fruits and vegetables that he had never seen before, and it all looked delicious.

"Shall we move to the table?" Max asked and got up from the bench. Victor didn't want to get up, he was more comfortable than he had ever been in his life, but eventually forced himself up and to the table. He was happy to discover that the chair at the far end of the table was nearly as comfortable as the bench. It was then that he noticed Jenny and Lenny were still standing at either end of the train.

"You two aren't going to sit and eat?" Victor asked, first looking at Jenny, then at Lenny.

"Oh uh, no. We will eat later. You enjoy," Lenny replied while holding back a smile. Victor did not know why they made that choice, but shrugged it off and turned to eat his fill.

"Shall we continue our previous conversation?" Max asked. Victor nodded his head.

"I won't bore you with specifics as I'm sure you wouldn't understand them, but yes, I own the power plant, and I allow the government to use it for a fee. It was the same agreement my family had with the United Nations government that controlled the world before Spidre came to power. And I am hoping it will be the same agreement, or maybe even better, under the next administration.

Victor stopped eating.

"What do you mean by next administration?" he asked.

"I mean that I see the writing on the walls," Max replied. "Spidre is losing his grasp on this world. Maybe you LO-ECs will take him down, or maybe it will be some other rebel group years down the line. But you have changed things. Spidre's iron grip is rusting, and is set to break. And whoever comes next, I want to make sure my assets are protected, and that I am in a better place under a new administration than I am now. The promise of better profits was the only reason we allowed Spidre to come to power in the first place."

"You... allowed Spidre to come to power?" Victor asked.

"Well, we certainly didn't stop him. Myself and the other

remaining industrial tycoons could have certainly made things more difficult for him if we wanted. But he promised us larger profits, more money, so we didn't get in his way."

"And so now that he is probably going to get taken down, and probably by us, you want to make another deal and betray Spidre," Victor said.

"Very savvy, I'm impressed," Max replied. "Spidre in control has yielded decent profits, but he is difficult to deal with. Once he gained full control of the world, and especially now that he has been in power for so long, he has adopted a 'my way or no way' mentality that we are not a fan of. I'd like to see someone more agreeable in his place."

"So, I see why you would want Spidre gone, but I don't see a reason why I should agree to this," Victor replied.

"I thought you might ask that. Jenny, if you would…" Max said over his shoulder. Jenny stepped around the counter and tapped a panel on the wall that was at her shoulder height. She then briskly walked to the other side of the train and stood next to Lenny as the counter she had been behind folded away into a wall compartment. Then, the walls on either side of the door Jenny had passed through to bring the food also folded away, revealing two large hidden compartments. Out of those compartments stepped two robotic forms, 8 feet tall and hulking in form. They clanked and whirred as they turned into the car. As they faced him, Victor immediately recognized the heavily armored facade and dread filled his mind as he leapt to his feet.

It was Tank, the colossal android that Victor, Edgar, Nadine, Naren, and Sera had barely managed to destroy as a team when they had first met. Only this time there were two of them, and Victor was alone while trapped on a moving train.

"I believe you have realized who these two are, and the situation you are in," Max said. As he spoke, the electric blades that made up the forearms of the two Tanks sparked and crackled as they activated.

CHAPTER TWELVE

"So here is how it's going to go," Max continued as the two Tanks stood motionless.

"If you try to attack me or either of these two androids, the fight will destroy this train and we will certainly all die. Since none of us want that, we will take this train to Praia. When we get there, you will see that these are not my only two androids, but in fact I have an entire army of them ready to answer to my beck and call."

There are more of these!? Victor thought to himself.

"I know what Praia's power plant provides power to, so I can figure your next move is to attack Spidre while the force field around his compound is down," Max said. "And as I stated before, I have no intention of stopping you. So, you will remain in Praia as my guest for two or three days while your teammates complete their portions of the plan. When that time comes, I will voluntarily cut the power coming from the Praia power plant and won't turn it back on until I hear from you or hear of Spidre's or your demise. If you try to run away before then or attempt to destroy the plant, I will immediately notify the military of your plan. If you stray from any of this and are foolish enough to not run, my army will end you. And in return for my help and my mercy, I ask for you to accept a new financial arrangement that is more beneficial to my bottom line. Do we have an agreement?"

Victor had calmed down some while Max was talking. He started seeing the full picture of the situation he was in.

"I agree," Victor said with a heavy sigh.

"A wise decision. You are clearly the smart one of your group," Max said. "Now, shall we return to our meal?"

Victor went back to his seat because it felt weird not to, but he was done eating.

"So, when would you need to leave?" Max asked.

"In the evening two days from now," Victor replied.

"Perfect. The mansion will essentially be yours to enjoy in that time. It will only be myself and the servant staff who will be there for your every need. Enjoy yourself," Max said with a big smile.

There was nothing Victor wanted more than to punch a hole straight through Max's face at that moment, but he knew that would mean his death and the derailment of their entire plan. Together they all waited out the next few tense, awkward minutes as the train approached Praia. The train slowed and eventually stopped, and the door they had entered the train through popped open. Then another door popped open, also at the rear of the car, but on the opposite side from the first door. Then the entire rear wall of the train popped open and a small automated platform with stairs slid in front of the new, larger exit. As Victor exited the car and walked down the stairs, he realized he was on a hillside that was covered in gorgeous, perfectly kept green grass. All over the grass, there was water spraying out of the ground in various spots. Past the hillside was what looked like an abandoned city, and past that was a megaskysraper complex of the sort that Victor was used to seeing, and next to that was an enormous dome that Victor had never seen before.

"Do you like my lawn? You wouldn't believe how expensive it is to keep those water sprinklers running, but it has to be done to keep the grass green," Max said as he, Lenny, and Jenny walked down the stairs.

"I'm more impressed with whatever that is," Victor said as he pointed at the giant dome.

"Ahh, that would be the powerplant," Max replied. By now the two Tank androids were lumbering out of the train, and Victor was sure to keep an eye on them. He was surprised when they stepped on to the platform and it was able to hold their weight without bowing. He continued to look at the surroundings and saw that the grass extended a few hundred more yards uphill from where they were standing. And on that section of the hillside were standing dozens, if not hundreds, of androids that appeared identical to the two he had just ridden to Praia with. His eyes then darted back to the other side of the tracks, where he saw what Max must have been referring to as his "small mansion." It was in fact a humongous five-story building made completely out of stone. It had huge glass windows all over and a two front doors that looked to be easily 15 feet high.

"And I see you noticed the quaint little spot I call home here," Max said. "Again, enjoy yourself. There are gardens in the back and all sorts of things to see inside. Lenny will always be nearby should you need anything. I will generally keep to myself unless you need me, but I would caution you that these two androids will be following me around for my own safety. I'm sure you understand."

"I do," Victor replied.

"Perfect. Lenny will see you to your room, then," Max said.

While this conversation was happening, Jenny had run ahead and opened the massive front doors. Max and his two androids walked in first and went off to the right down a huge, high, grand hallway. Again, everything was colored gold and red, and paintings and various other art pieces dotted the walls. As Victor and Lenny walked in, Victor saw a giant staircase in front of him, and another large hallway to the left, toward which Lenny guided him. At the end of the hall, they made it to the correct room and Lenny opened the door for Victor.

In contrast to the rest of the house, the room was a dark purple instead of red, and had dark wood accents rather than the gold that was all over everything else. In the center of the room was the biggest bed that Victor had ever seen. The other three walls all had giant windows, each giving a different view of outside. There were tables and very fluffy chairs at various spots in the room, and also larger pieces of furniture with drawers that Victor assumed were for clothes, although he didn't have nearly enough spare clothing with him to fill them.

"You have a personal bathroom through that door there," Lenny said, pointing at a door that was on the same wall as the door through which they had entered. "I can draw a bath for you if you'd like and can fetch a change of clothes."

"Uhh, I'll handle the bath myself. But I will take you up on that offer for new clothes, " Victor said.

"At once, sir," Lenny said.

"No suits though," Victor said. Lenny cracked a smile.

"That is not a problem," Lenny replied.

"So, are you and Jenny related or something?" Victor asked. Lenny was briefly stunned by the random question.

"No… why do you ask?"

"Well, two of my friends are Naren and Nadine," Victor said. "They have similar names and are related, and Lenny and Jenny are even closer names so…"

"Oh no, no, it is nothing like that," Lenny said. "You see Mr. Bennington had the nickname 'Benny' when he was in school. It was a shortened version of his last name. So since he was known as Benny, he only hired servants that had the same 'enny' ending to their name. He found it more aesthetically pleasing that way. There is myself, Jenny, Penny, Kenny…"

"Wait, are you being serious right now?" Victor asked.

"Yes, sir, I am," Lenny replied.

"God, your boss is a fucking weirdo," Victor replied, causing Lenny to nearly choke holding back laughter.

"He is… eccentric," Lenny eventually replied after composing himself. Silence lingered for a few seconds after that.

"Well, I guess I'd better go get…" Lenny started.

"Hey, I'm sorry for earlier," Victor interrupted again. Lenny seemed more surprised by this than by the random question about his and Jenny's name.

"For grabbing you and hurting you, I mean," Victor clarified. "I know it might be hard to believe, but I actually do try very hard not to harm innocent people. And you seem innocent enough in all this."

"I… don't know what to say…" Lenny began, but then immediately regained his composure and cleared his throat.

"No apology is necessary sir, I'm sure I would have reacted similarly were I in your position," Lenny said.

"I guess," Victor said.

"Well, I guess I'd better go get that change of clothes for you," Lenny said.

"Thank you, Lenny," Victor said softly.

"My pleasure, Victor." Lenny replied as he turned toward the door with a wide grin on his face.

CHAPTER THIRTEEN

"I don't see it," Victor said.

"See what?" Lenny asked.

"The number five. Where is it?" Victor inquired in turn.

"No, no, that's just the title of the painting, the label. There is no actual number five painted, at least not intentionally," Lenny replied as they both gazed at a giant painting on the walls of a gallery in the mansion's upper levels.

"So, was it the fifth painting this Jack guy made?" Victor asked.

"Jackson. And no, probably not," Lenny responded.

"So then why the hell is it called number five?!" Victor exclaimed, making Lenny chuckle.

"So this type of painting is called abstract expressionism," Lenny explained. "It's called number five so that people have some way to identify it in conversation, but that's it. It doesn't have a real title, because the subject of the painting is whatever the viewer imagines it to be."

Victor stared at the painting in silence for a long time, and Lenny stared at Victor, eager to see a reaction.

"It looks like a bird's nest," Victor eventually replied. Lenny choked back laughter.

"So it's not just about what you see the painting to be, but how it makes you feel. What emotions stir inside you as you look at the paint lines?"

Victor stayed silent for even longer this time, keenly focused on the multicolored lines in front of him.

"It makes me feel confused," Victor confessed. Lenny burst out laughing.

"Why is that funny?!" Victor exclaimed.

"I am sorry, that was rude of me," Lenny replied as he composed himself. "I'm just so used to Mr. Bennington and his friends having these long-winded, complicated, measured interpretations that I can't make sense of. It was delightfully refreshing to hear such a simple and valid response."

"Well, what do you see when you look at the painting?" Victor asked.

"I like to think of it as layers of understanding," Lenny replied as he looked ahead. "The red represents the parts of our world that I fully understand, or at least am comfortable in my knowledgeable of them. The yellow is things I know about but could know more. Black and grey are things I know nothing about. And the white is things I know little about but want to understand better." Lenny's eyes flicked from the painting back to Victor as he concluded his last sentence.

"But there is so little red!" Victor responded. "If that's how little you know, well, then I am fucked."

"Why do you feel that way?"

"There is so much I don't understand about what's going on here, and I'm not just talking about this painting."

"What is it you want clarification about? I might be able to help," Lenny said. Victor took a deep breath.

"I don't understand how the fuck Max has so much money but I have never heard about him before in my life. I don't understand how you know so much about these things that have nothing to do with actual life. And I don't understand how or why you are working for Max when you seem so nice and he seems like such a prick."

"Hmmm…" Lenny replied. "So, I don't have all the details on how Mr. Bennington is so rich, but I know the basics."

"I'll take it," Victor replied, making Lenny smile.

"So, Mr. Bennington did not gain much of the wealth himself. Long ago, his family was contracted to build the power plant and the government paid them to do it. I am not sure exactly why they never fully took over the plant afterward, but I suspect the plant either requires too much very specific knowledge to run, or that Mr. Bennington's family blackmailed the government in some way, made it so that they had to stay involved or the plant would shut down. Either way, that's how it played out and continues the same to this day. Spidre can't just kill him and risk losing the plant, but he can re-work the deal as he sees fit, and Mr. Bennington has little choice but to accept since Spidre is the only customer."

"So that's why Max wants Spidre gone. Got it," Victor said. Lenny nodded in reply.

"But where does the government get the money to pay Max?" Victor asked.

"Oh. Taxes," Lenny replied simply. Victor raised an eyebrow.

"Wait, did your learning curriculum not teach you about taxes?" Lenny asked.

"Oh. I only did that for two years," Victor replied. Lenny squinted his eyes in confusion at first, and then went pale.

"Victor, what the hell have you been through?" Lenny asked.

Victor then proceeded to fill Lenny in on everything that happened in his life: his parents being murdered when he was eight years old, his solo cross-continental journey to evade Spidre's forces, and the twenty years he spent alone in the woods, surviving on what he could forage, hunt, and steal. When Victor concluded, tears were welling in Lenny's eyes.

"Oh, Victor. I am so sorry. You went through so much…" Lenny said.

"Thank you. But yeah, so all of that is why I don't know taxes," Victor replied, making Lenny chuckle through tears.

"So, most of the world, I guess all of it besides maybe the places that are rebelling, operates in a 'work optional' way. Everyone, even all those folks who don't work, are guaranteed an apartment in a megaskyscraper, the basic furnishings to live in that apartment, food from the dispensaries, water, clothes, a mobile, and a basic education. If someone wants to get something besides these guaranteed essentials, they can choose to get a job. They get paid for that job and spend that money on stuff. Every time they buy stuff, a small amount of that money they spend gets taken by the government to pay for the stuff that's guaranteed to everyone. That money the government takes is called taxes."

"And some of that small amount of money also gets given by the government to Max for the 'service' of getting power," Victor said.

"Exactly!" Lenny replied. "Mr. Bennington also has other businesses he owns that make money when people buy stuff. But someone who buys his stuff wouldn't know or particularly care who he is, because why would that matter if they're getting the item they want? And if those folks have no reason to know who he is, then the folks who don't work and can't buy stuff will have even less of a reason to know about him."

"Yeah, that makes sense," Victor said. "I guess it would be weird to know about someone just cuz they have lots of money."

"Yes. Quite weird," Lenny said.

"So how did you find out about him and start working for him?" Victor asked.

"Hmm, where to start with that..." Lenny pondered for a moment as he scratched his chin.

"Ok, so if a person decides they want to work, the government sets them up with a little extra education to prep them for an aptitude test. A person takes that test and then gets a choice of jobs based on what they're good at. My parents worked, and wanted me to work when I became an adult, so they paid for extra education for me. That way when I took the aptitude test, I would be more likely to get better scores in lots of categories and a better choice of jobs that pay well. I did very well on the test, well enough that some of the tycoons took notice. Mr. Bennington especially liked me because of the affinity for my name that we talked about yesterday, and offered me a big salary, which I accepted."

"So that's why you work for Max? Just cuz it's a lot of money?" Victor asked.

"That's an overly simplified explanation," Lenny responded. "I think we've been staring at this painting long enough, how about we go downstairs and take a walk in the gardens?" Lenny asked.

"Uhh, sure?" Victor replied, and they both turned for the stairs. After descending the main staircase, Victor followed Lenny to the rear of the building, through a large dining-room space, and through glass doors to the outside. There were bushes and trees everywhere, all of different heights and with different colors of flowers.

"This place is really, really, green," Victor commented as he looked around. Lenny chuckled. As they stepped off of a stone walkway and onto the grass, Victor felt mist in the air cling to his face. He assumed this was more of the water Max had mentioned that had to constantly run to keep the plants alive.

"So, what I'm about to tell you, I have never told anyone here. I wanted to come outside because I don't want anyone knowing my future plans," Lenny said as he took a deep breath. Victor's heart raced.

"It isn't the money itself that I care about, it is what the money can provide," Lenny said. "My parents worked to provide a better life for me, and they succeeded. I want to build on that, earn enough that when I start a family of my own, they can have more than just what the government provides without having to work themselves. The best of both worlds."

"Wow," Victor replied, wide eyed in awe. "But would that mean you would eventually leave your job here?"

"Yes," Lenny replied. "Working for Max has been fine. Most days it's just getting him food or drinks or talking about art with other rich people," Lenny said. "But you saw for yourself, he does not care about us. Max was ready to let you kill me to serve his own goals. I wouldn't go so far as to call him evil, but he cares about little else besides himself and his wealth. That is not an environment in which to bring up a family in the long-term, no matter how luxurious it is."

"So, when do you plan to leave this place?" Victor asked.

"When I find a person worth leaving for," Lenny replied as he stared directly into Victor's eyes and a gentle smile came to his face.

"Well, I hope you find that person even... wait a minute," Victor began to reply, then remembered some past conversations he had had with Sera.

"Are, are you doing that thing?" Victor asked.

"What thing?" Lenny replied.

"Oh, what the heck was it called… Fleering? Flooring? Flirting? Flirting! Are you flirting me?"

"Flirting with you," Lenny replied with another chuckle. "And I guess that would depend on if it's working."

"Shit, umm…" Victor stumbled with his words as he turned bright red.

"A no is an ok response…" Lenny said.

"No! I mean, fuck!" Victor replied. "Not that kind of no. I'm not saying no. Sorry, I'm not good at this stuff… You're sweet, and nice. But we just met. How do you know already that I'm the right person?"

"I don't. But I'd like to find out if you are or not," Lenny said.

"I would like that, too," Victor replied as his heart pounded in his chest. All sorts of thoughts of a potential future raced through his head before he shook himself back into reality.

"I'm being hunted, Lenny. The whole world's army wants me dead. How would that work?"

"I could hide you. Find a comfortable place where you can live that is outside of the governments prying eyes. Hell, I bet I could even convince Max to let you stay here."

"What?!" Victor exclaimed.

"You are the most powerful person I have ever met. I am sure that is true for Max as well," Lenny said. "Convincing him to let you stay here as security would be an easy sell to him. We stay here and get to know each other better, and if things go well then…"

"Does Max need me? What about the androids?" Victor asked. Lenny stayed dead silent. He didn't say a word and didn't need to. Victor already had suspicions about the androids, and Lenny's silence confirmed it.

Victor dropped his head. Lenny's plan sounded incredible. It pained him to turn it down.

"I can't stay," Victor responded with his eyes shut tight. He could sense the deflation of excitement coming from Lenny.

"I want to, I just can't. At least, not yet," Victor continued as he raised his head and met Lenny's stare again.

"I understand," Lenny replied. "But your fight will not go on forever. Whenever it finally ends, I hope you will try and come find me."

CHAPTER FOURTEEN

The next day was uneventful. Victor wore his newly acquired clothes and walked around the mansion and garden, looking at things and occasionally talking to Lenny about them. At one point, he walked up the hill to check out the army of Tanks and confirmed they were the same as the ones he saw on the train. As the morning of the day he was supposed to leave came, he asked Lenny if he could meet Max for breakfast.

Max agreed, and they met in a dining hall that was past the staircase on the first floor. Victor got there first and began eating his fill, and Max arrived about ten minutes later with his androids in tow.

"Good morning, Victor," Max said as he entered.

"Hi Max," Victor replied in between mouthfuls of food.

"So I must admit curiosity is getting the better of me. I never expected to be asked to join you for a meal. What motivates this?" Max asked.

"Well, I was thinking about the agreement we made, and I had ideas on how to improve it," Victor said.

"Is that right?" Max asked.

"Yes," Victor. "But first, I wanted to verify something."

Victor threw his chair out from behind him and turned into a blur as he raced across the dining hall, straight towards the android to Max's right. As he came close, Victor threw a left-handed punch as hard as he could straight into the abdomen of his targeted Tank, and his fist effortlessly pierced the armor and buried itself among the electronics inside. He grabbed hold of them and pulled his arm out of the hole. In pulling his arm back he nearly ripped Tank's entire side out, and the android immediately powered down and fell backward.

"So, I was right. You have stupid fucking copies, not real Tanks," Victor said, and immediately dashed out of the dining room, past the staircase, and splintered the front doors as he burst through it. He sprinted as fast as his feet could take him down the hill, through the abandoned old city, and to the powerplant. As he approached one of the doors to the plant, he barely slowed down as he slammed into it and wrenched it from its hinges. This was finally the part of the plan where he actually knew what he was doing. He ran down hallways until he saw exactly what Symon and Naren had described to him, which May had described to them months before. In the floor of a fairly large room on the ground level was a six-foot wide cable that had thousands of smaller wires running to it. He threw an air burst down at this and severed all the connections. He had just disabled the main electric cable that ran out of the powerplant and, eventually, to Spidre's compound. The lights around him dimmed as he ran back through the hallways and out of the building. He ran back to the mansion and saw that by then, Max had come outside with his one functional android. Lenny and Jenny were there too.

"What did you just do!?" Max screamed.

"Exactly what I came here to do. I disabled the supermassive powerplant," Victor responded.

"You agreed you wouldn't!" Max kept shouting.

"I lied," Victor replied.

"Kill him! All of you!" Max bellowed, and the android behind him clunked forward. The dozens on the hillside came to life as well and turned to join the fight. Victor ran forward, grabbed the android near Max at its wide waist, and sank his hands into the metal. He twisted his body while still grabbing hold and ripped the top of the android clear from its legs. He tossed the torso to the side and ran uphill towards the other androids. One by one and with the slightest of effort, Victor tore them all apart. The androids were slow, weak, and utterly helpless to stop the speed and strength Victor had in spades. The hillside roared with noise as metal shrieked and crumpled and wires twisted and snapped. In a matter of minutes, what once had been a metal army was a mound of scrap metal so large it hid the green grass of the hillside. When Victor was finished, he casually walked back to Max.

"You!" Max hollered with madness in his eyes.

"I am going to tell the military where you are at once!" Max continued.

"Go ahead, it doesn't matter if they know where I am now," Victor replied. "My friends are either finished disabling the other powerplants or will be shortly. There is nothing the military can do now to stop us."

"You! You! I'll…" Max started.

"You aren't going to do fucking shit!" Victor screamed as loudly as he could, scaring Max so much that he lost his footing.

"A few days ago, you called me 'the smart one of the group' and clearly meant to make me feel insulted by it," Victor said. "I don't know if I'm the smartest in my group, they're a bunch of geniuses, but I'm certainly smarter than Mr. Maximillion Bennington the Fourteenth."

Max's eyes went wide.

"Your name is not hard to pronounce, but your ego was easy to bruise, and your plan was easy to see holes in after just a second of thinking about it. Only a fucking moron would hear that someone planned to destroy their expensive building, and then take them within mere miles of that same fucking building. I'll admit that your little stunt with the androids shook me at first, but let me clue you in to something. Tank, the real one, he didn't clink and clank. He didn't slowly lumber around. And when I fought him, he was so heavy that he made a giant transport shake just by jumping off of it. But your pathetic copies didn't even make your train platform bow when they stepped on it."

"Good, great, grand, you figured everything out. You accomplished your goal, so what the fuck are you still doing here!?" Max replied.

"Oh, my plans changed slightly," Victor replied. "Your Tank copies were pathetic, but in the hands of a non-moron, having the ability to make many Tanks could be dangerous. So, you are going to tell me where they are made, and I am going to destroy them. I know it's near here somewhere."

"How do you know that?" Max asked.

"Because you didn't know I was going to Praia until I told you. Meaning you were able to get dozens of robots here to your hillside in about an hour. That means they were close by," Victor said.

"Fine, but I'm not going to tell you where it is. You're so fast, find it yourself." Max replied.

"Not enough time for that," Victor said, and ran over to Lenny and Jenny. He grabbed them both, ran to the hillside far from the mansion, and placed them both down carefully. He then ran back to Max and while doing so, threw an air burst at Max's golden train. The trains roof was shredded into thousands of pieces while the parts closer to the tracks exploded into a hissing sparking inferno.

"What are you doing!?" Max cried.

"The mansion is next unless you tell me what I want to know," Victor replied.

"You wouldn't!" Max said. At that Victor ran inside and first came out with Kenny, then Penny, and placed them both next to Jenny and Lenny. When he was certain the building was empty, he ran back to Max and threw three air bursts at the mansion. The first careened into the top of the building and it immediately began to crumble. The second hit the bottom of the building and it crumbled even faster. The third hit all of the crumbling stone and threw it hundreds of feet away across the garden and hillside behind it.

"The powerplant is next," Victor said.

"Are you crazy!?" Max screamed. "If you destroy the plant, it will cause a nuclear meltdown!"

"I'm pretty sure I can outrun that," Victor replied. "Hell, I bet I can even carry all four 'ennys' and still outrun it. You won't, though, and neither will that facility that makes Tanks."

Max stayed silent. Victor turned and held both of his hands high over his head, preparing to unleash the mightiest air burst he had ever attempted. He actually wasn't sure if it would reach the plant, but it didn't matter.

"It's just down the hill!" Max finally spat out.

"There is an industrial park down there, and the building that manufactures androids is a red concrete building."

"Of course it's red," Victor said. He darted down the hill and found the building with little effort. He kicked the door in and briefly looked inside to confirm what Max had told him. Sure enough, there were conveyor belts and robotic arms all carrying pieces of what would eventually be fully fledged androids. Victor ran back a few yards, threw some air bursts to bring the building down, then threw several more for good measure to make sure everything was destroyed beyond salvage. After that, he ran back to Max.

"What I said at breakfast is still true, I want to discuss our previous agreement," Victor said. He then snatched Max by the jaw and held him aloft, just like he had done with Lenny a few days earlier.

"You betrayed the United Nations, and you are betraying Spidre. What reason would I have to believe you wouldn't do the same to us in the future?" Victor said.

"I promise I…" Max sputtered.

"Shut the fuck up!" Victor screamed. "Here is the new deal. I assume we will need you if we do take down Spidre and form a new government to lead Earth. That is the only reason I am allowing you to live. You will repair your powerplant, and if Spidre dies you will use it to provide power to the world. It will be up to someone besides me to decide how or how much you get paid for this 'service'. But you will never do anything to directly or indirectly bring harm to me or my friends, including making androids or showing someone else how to do it. And if at any point I feel you have gone against this agreement, I will find you and kill you, and as I just showed you there is absolutely nothing you can do to stop me. Do we have a deal?"

Max did his best attempt to nod while Victor held his jaw, and Victor let him go. He turned back towards the servants who were still standing on the hillside.

"Goodbye, '-ennys'," he said, but was looking squarely at Lenny

when he said it. Lenny let the faintest smile loose while the rest of
the servants stood dumbfounded. Victor then briefly looked at the
sky to figure out which way he needed to run, and took off to the
west across the Atlantic Ocean.

CHAPTER FIFTEEN

Of all the routes each LO-EC had to take, Edgar's was arguably the most complicated. Besides Symon, he was the only one of the group who was functionally landbound. There was no cutting across oceans or flying over mountains for him, he was stuck to wherever the two wheels of an Elcycle could go. That meant cutting across clear, flat areas of land when he could, and sticking to roadways whenever the earth rose or fell. The problem with the trip down to Quito was that there was one area, where Central and South America met, where no roads had ever been built and where there was still thick rainforest covering the ground.

Figuring out a way to program the elcycle's autonav to get through this area was difficult, even for an expert like Symon, but they did finally find one path that worked. Edgar would first cut across the desert for some time, then onto roads that brought him to the Pacific coast in Mexico. He'd stay on the roads along the coast for a long time until he intersected a TCT line that crossed over the Gulf of Panama and into South America. That TCT line was the only structure that spanned across the two continents. He would have to follow that line as it became a bridge in some places and a tunnel in others until he got to the next road. According to the autonav on the elcycle, that road was navigable and eventually made it to Quito. However, the start of the road was still in the rainforest, and according to Symon that area was notorious for harboring various groups that were trying to stay off the world government's radar. Symon doubted anything in there could stop Edgar, but it could delay him, and his margin for error was only a few hours.

Having said his goodbyes to Nadine, Edgar took a deep breath, threw a leg over his elcycle, and took off towards the south. The first section of his journey was supposed to be the easiest, and it was. He traveled through the desert without issue, and eventually met up with the Pacific coast roads. He stopped at that point to eat and rest a little. He knew the only chances he would have to stop would be on this trip south. After he took out the power plant in Quito, he would essentially have to drive non-stop and as fast as he safely could to get to San Francisco in time.

After resting, Edgar started his road-bound part of the journey. He had to be a little more careful here. The route he was taking avoided any cities with a megaskyscaper complex, but it was theoretically possible for him to run into military vehicles doing supply runs or some other operation. Fortunately, it was nothing but open deserted road until, after a day and a half, he finally arrived at the junction with the TCT line. Symon had chosen this spot specifically because it was one of the few areas where the TCT was at ground level and had a section exposed to open air. Edgar waited until late afternoon, when this section of the TCT had no trains running till the next morning, then slid himself and the elcycle under a barricade and started the next phase of the journey, riding the elcycle on the single four-foot-wide rail that the TCT traversed.

As morning neared, Edgar could see that the turn off of the TCT line was coming, but the area was pitch black, not a single source of light besides the moon and stars. He trusted that the autonav would do its thing, and sure enough it guided him off the rail and onto a small road about ten feet below.

This road was cracked and crumbling even more than those he had used previously, but it was passable. However, as dawn broke, Edgar had to slow to a stop when the road was blocked by what looked like a military personnel transport, though something was different about it. It somehow looked clunky, like it was an older, less-well-designed version. As he stopped, four men came around from the other side of the transport in military armor with machine guns attached at the arms. Edgar immediately recognized the armor as an older version that he hadn't seen since he was young.

"Quién eres? Què estàs haciendo aquí?" one of the men yelled, but it was in another language that Edgar not only couldn't speak, but he wasn't sure he had ever even heard it before.

"I'm sorry, I don't understand," Edgar replied.

"Quièn eres tu y que estas haciendo aquí!?" another man yelled even louder.

"I don't... do any of you speak... normal..?" Edgar asked, having never encountered someone who spoke another language before.

"Ingles?" One man asked another.

"Ingles..." the other said with a heavy sigh.

"What you want?!" the same man yelled at Edgar.

"I need to pass. I go to Quito," Edgar replied, trying to keep his words as simple as possible.

All four men pointed their guns at Edgar.

"You leave. Go back now!" the same man yelled.

"No," Edgar replied as he took his hands off his elcycle's grips. He activated his powers and a four-foot-long blue blade extended out of his right hand. The four men's eyes went wide.

"Move!" Edgar yelled. The four men lowered their guns but began to look at each other with widened eyes.

"Uno momento! You stay! Uno momento!" said the same man that had previously been telling Edgar to leave. Two of the other men ran off into the forest.

"Brenda! Brenda!" he heard the two men yelling.

"I need to go!" Edgar yelled. As he did, he saw a flash of blue light jump out of the forest and stop on the road in between Edgar and the transport. When it stopped moving, Edgar saw it was a woman who was at least a foot shorter than him and wide in stature. Her arms were arched in front of her chest, and they both had enormous blue streaks of light coming off of them starting at the wrist and wrapping all the way back past her shoulders.

"Holy shit, you're a LO-EC!" Edgar said.

"Holy shit, you speak English!" the woman said, and deactivated her powers. Edgar could see her microtransformers, the part of LO-EC tech where their energy emanated from, were dotted all over each arm. Edgar assumed that each of them could emit energy, and that all together they formed those long blades that covered her entire arm. Edgar also deactivated his power and his own blade of energy disappeared.

"Is English what you call speaking normally?" Edgar asked.

"You speak English, they all speak Spanish. It's a long story. I'm Brenda," the woman said.

"I'm Edgar," Edgar said.

"Why on earth are you here?" Brenda asked.

"It's a long story," Edgar said with a smirk.

"Give me the short version," Brenda asked.

"I just need to get to Quito. And I'm kind of in a rush, which is a shame because I'd love to know how on earth you ended up out here," Edgar said.

"My family came here to hide after the military started murdering all LO-ECs and we joined up with this paramilitary group, of whom you have already met some members," Brenda said, gesturing at the four men around her.

"You are better at the short version of things than I am," Edgar said, getting a smirk out of Brenda.

"You aren't with one of the other paramilitary groups, are you?" Brenda asked.

Edgar had to think about that. "I guess we technically could be considered paramilitary, but not from anywhere around here, and my fight is with the world government, not you all."

Brenda glared at Edgar for a moment.

"If I hear about you causing trouble or if I see you on this road again, you and I will have issues," Brenda said.

"There's a problem there. I am going to Quito specifically to cause trouble, and I need to take this road back north when I'm done," Edgar replied, and Brenda threw her arms up in frustration.

"This is what I get for trying to be reasonable. Come with us now or die where you stand," Brenda said, and as she did, she activated her powers again, which in turn caused her men to point their guns at Edgar.

Edgar thought for a moment. Even with this new development, he was pretty sure of his ability to run or fight his way out of the situation. On the other hand, he still had a few hours of spare time, and a chance to learn more about Brenda and her operation that he might never get again.

"Am I safe to assume you all are not allied with Spidre?" Edgar asked.

"Spidre? The world leader Spidre?" Brenda asked in turn.

"Yes," Edgar said.

"Fuck no," Brenda replied.

"Good. I will come with you, then," he replied as he swung his leg over the elcycle to dismount. "Will my ride be safe here or should I bring it?"

"Your cycle belongs to us now," Brenda replied. Edgar's expression turned grim as he let go of the handlebars.

"I am sorry to be so blunt here, but if you or any of your people try to touch my elcycle, I will kill all of you," Edgar said.

"Are you seriously making threats right now?!" Brenda exclaimed. Edgar activated the energy in both of his hands and the blue aura extended out to each of his sides.

"It is not a threat," Edgar replied. "I am coming with you because I choose to. If I choose to leave instead, you will not be able to stop me."

Brenda seemed at a loss for words for a moment, but then a coy smile crept to her face.

"Baja su armas!" Brenda announced to her allies, and they lowered their guns.

"If you are so confident in yourself, then let's bet on it," Brenda said to Edgar. "You and me fight, but not to kill. If you win, I will let you go do whatever you have planned. If I win, you stay here and fight for me, and I keep your bike."

Edgar's heart raced at the prospect of getting to spar with a new superpowered LO-EC, but luckily his mind stayed focused.

"I want to fight, but I have a better plan regardless which of us win," Edgar said, raising one of Brenda's eyebrows.

"I keep my elcycle, and you tell me more of your story. And in return, I will help you take over this entire region before sunset."

Once again, Brenda seemed flustered momentarily.

"You cannot guarantee such things," Brenda said.

"I can," Edgar replied.

"How?" Brenda asked.

"Because before nightfall, the weapons and supplies of the Quito regiment will belong to you," Edgar said.

CHAPTER SIXTEEN

"So, you're crazy. Got it." Brenda responded.

"Yeah, maybe," Edgar responded. "But that doesn't mean my plan won't work."

"You cannot fight a whole army!" Brenda exclaimed.

"Why not? I did it a few times already," Edgar replied, and a wave of understanding fell across Brenda's face.

"You are with that group that attacked Chicago," she said.

"Holy shit, you all heard about that even out here?" Edgar asked.

"We have our ways of gathering information," Brenda replied. "But where is the rest of your team?"

"Fighting in other areas of the world," Edgar said. Brenda nodded gently and finally deactivated her powers.

"El no es una amenaza para nosotros," Brenda yelled to her allies, and they lowered their guns.

"I just told them you aren't a threat. Do not make me a liar," Brenda told Edgar.

"Thank you," Edgar said.

"I still have questions. Answer them while we walk to camp," Brenda continued. Edgar nodded.

He walked his elcycle off the road and followed Brenda through the jungle on well-cut paths. As they walked, he filled her in on everything that happened since the assault on Chicago, and the plan they were currently executing to finally bring Spidre down for good.

"So, my friends are all at the other corners of the world disabling the power plants that power the forcefield around Spidre's compound. I need to go to Quito to do that same thing, then haul ass to San Francisco so all of us can attack Spidre head on," Edgar concluded.

"But how do you know if your allies were successful in their fights?" Brenda asked.

"I don't," Edgar replied. "I just do my part and have faith that they'll do the same."

"So, all of you are crazy. Not just you." Brenda said, causing Edgar to crack a smile.

"How do you, any of you, expect to fight an entire regiment by yourself?" she asked.

"Oh, I don't know what everyone else's ideas are. But my plan is to fight as little as possible. Smash a door or wall at the plant, fight my way to the room I need, destroy that room, fight my way out."

"It can't be that easy," Brenda replied.

"Why can't it?" Edgar asked.

"Because if it was, someone else would have tried by now," Brenda said.

"Have you tried?" Edgar asked.

"Of course not!" Brenda responded.

"Well, you and those like you are the only ones with any reason to try and any ability to do so. But my motivation is more defined, and I have a couple key advantages that you don't."

"Oh? Like what?" Brenda asked through a scowl.

"This elcycle, for starters." Edgar said as he patted the handlebars. "I can get away fast and without needing another source of power to keep my ride moving. My other advantage is that when I make my getaway, I'm not going back to a nearby jungle that the local forces can search if given the motivation."

"You're right about the elcycle, not the jungle," Brenda replied. Edgar glanced over to her, prompting her to keep explaining.

"The military has come for us many times. Even before my family joined this group, the peacekeepers did not like that there was armed paramilitary hiding in the jungle and occasionally came to get us. And each time we have either evaded their searches or fought them off."

"So, you can't fight them out in the city, but the second they step into your jungle, they lose the advantage," Edgar said.

"Exactly. Fighting in here is an entirely different thing, and we are the experts."

"But why have your allies been here so long?" Edgar asked. "Are they all LO-ECs?"

"People have always had reasons to hide from the government. Some are more valid than others, and some are more violent. But I am the only LO-EC in this group," Brenda said. But there was something about Brenda's phrasing that caught Edgar's attention.

"Only? So your parents…"

"I said we fought off the peacekeepers when they came. I didn't say we didn't have casualties from doing so".

"I'm sorry," Edgar replied.

"It was a while ago. Can we change the subject?" Brenda asked.

"Of course," Edgar said. He could sympathize with how Brenda was feeling.

"You said you were the only LO-EC in this group. Does that

mean there are others in this jungle?"

"Yes. Many families like mine fled to the jungle when the army came for us. I'm not sure how many survived till now, and I surely don't know about all of them. But there are at least ten others with powers like ours and a handful more that are stronger than normal people but that's it. All of us are leaders or key enforcers of our groups."

"But none of you are allied with one another?" Edgar asked.

"Why would I ally with those power-hungry fuckers?" Brenda snapped back. "They only understand strength and fear. Reason and strategy are lost on them."

"So, it sounds like if you were to gain more power, say by taking over Quito and taking control of the army's weapons, you would have something else to gain, too," Edgar replied and glanced in Brenda's direction. Brenda gave the faintest of glances back at him.

"We are here," Brenda said just as the jungle opened up some. The area they had entered was still forested, but some areas were clear of trees while others had cloth tents and small huts in place of greenery. Some of the enclosures were supported by the backs of old, beaten-up electric vehicles.

"Wow," Edgar said as he glanced around. "What are those?" Edgar asked as he pointed at several large black squares that were lying on the ground in one of the cleared areas.

"Solar panels," Brenda replied. Edgar raised an eyebrow and cocked his head to the side.

"Really old tech," Brenda explained further. "We power our vehicles with them. They're slow as fuck to charge but they only need sunlight to do it."

"They make electricity out of the sun?!" Edgar exclaimed, wanting to know more, but he was cut off by others approaching from within the camp.

"Quien carajo es este?" someone said to Brenda.

"No importa. El no es una amenza y no se queda," Brenda replied.

"Por qué estás el aquí?" the same person said much more forcefully.

"Lo voy a averiguar y creo que puedas tener otras información que sea útil para nosotros," Brenda said calmly. "Lo voy a traer a mi carpa, no lo moleste."

"Come with me. Bring your cycle," Brenda said to Edgar.

"Everything ok?" Edgar asked.

"It will be if you follow me right now," she responded. They walked through the camp until they reached a large beige tent and went inside. The tent was mostly bare besides another tarp laid out across the ground and a bed roll in the corner. Brenda walked to the far end of the tent and sat on the tarp. She motioned for Edgar to sit across from her, and he did.

"So you really think we can take over Quito?" she asked.

"As long as you have faith in your group's ability to fight, yes," Edgar replied.

"They can fight, but not a whole army."

"They wouldn't have to fight an army. You and I would do most of the hard work."

"How?"

"We invade their headquarters and cut down everyone we can."

Brenda stayed silent. Edgar took this to mean he should explain further.

"When my allies and I attacked Chicago, I cleared out an entire building full of peacekeepers with the help of one other LO-EC with powers. Granted, she is the best hand-to-hand fighter I have ever met, but Chicago's forces were also among the most feared."

"How did you do it?"

"Others in my group have the ability to fly. They took the both of us up to the roof and we worked our way down floor by floor, tearing apart any soldiers that dared to try and stop us."

"We cannot get to the roof now."

"We don't need to. You and I attack the front door head on. With our powers and strength, we'll have the upper hand fighting in close quarters. Once the ground floor is clear, your soldiers come in and you work your way up the building with them until everyone is dead."

"Wait. You said me and my soldiers. Meaning you aren't going to help us clear the upper floors?"

"I told you, I have to disable the power plant and then head full speed back to San Francisco. An assault on a headquarters could take hours and use up energy I can't spare. I can help you get in the door, after that you're on your own."

Brenda glared at Edgar.

"Controlling the bottom floor is all you need my help with anyway. The peacekeepers will be trapped with no escape. You can take your time with the assault from that point on."

"Even if I agree with you, my group won't. Some stranger comes in, talks to me for a little while, and all of a sudden we're mounting an assault on a city? They will think I've gone crazy and that you're some kind of spy trying to get us all killed."

Edgar thought for a moment in silence.

"Maybe think about it like this," he started again. "I'm going to Quito whether you're coming or not. Maybe I take down the power plant, maybe I don't. Maybe me and my friends kill Spidre when we reunite, or maybe we fail. But even if we all die, Spidre's reign is going to come to an end soon. He is losing his grip on power. You said you get info about the rest of the world, so I'm sure you can see what I'm telling you."

"Yes, I can see it," Brenda admitted.

"So, when he falls, the world army will seem weak. Others with some power will try to take advantage and gain an upper hand. And your rival paramilitary groups sound like exactly that type of people."

Brenda went wide eyed as the realization dawned on her.

"Whoever is the first to take over Quito will control this whole region," she said frantically.

"And you have a one-time advantage of getting my help to do that right now," Edgar responded.

Brenda held her head aloft between her hands and stared at the floor, deep in thought.

"Holy fuck, you're right. But how do I convince…" she trailed off, then abruptly sat straight up and looked directly at Edgar.

"Fight me," Brenda said,

"What!?"

"Fight me. Fight me in front of everyone. Prove you are the badass you claim to be. It's the only thing that might convince everyone to follow you. If you lose, then you aren't worth following into a plan so foolish anyway."

Edgar shrugged.

"Ok, sure," he replied.

CHAPTER SEVENTEEN

"Reúne a todos alrededor el claro más grande! Este tonto cree que puedes peliar conmigo!" Brenda barked at one of her soldiers. Within two minutes, the entire camp was encircling the largest cleared area and she and Edgar faced each other in the center. They each activated their powers and squared up, waiting for the other to make their first move. After a few moments, Brenda leapt towards Edgar while bringing her left arm all the way across her body. She swung her blade of bio-energy in a wide arc as she came within striking distance. But Edgar had already brought his right hand up to block, and their blades briefly bounced off of each other before they began pushing against one another.

"That sure looked like you were trying to kill me," Edgar said through gritted teeth. Brenda didn't respond. Edgar looked past her arm and could see she was entirely focused on this first test of Edgar's strength. Seeing this, Edgar already knew the fight would be his. He deactivated the blade on his left arm. Brenda noticed but couldn't react before Edgar leaned in with his blocking hand and threw Brenda off of him. She went wide eyed and immediately went for another swinging blow with the same arm. This time

Edgar deflected the hit towards his right before Brenda came to a full stop. She stumbled while throwing her arm up to stop the momentum, and Edgar took the opportunity to drive his shoulder into her exposed left side.

Brenda took three steps to steady herself and then grunted in frustration. She charged in again, but Edgar was plenty ready. She had barely started moving, and he was already bringing his de-powered left arm up in line with her head. He activated his powers, and the blade came within inches of Brenda's face before she stopped and backtracked. She threw her hand up to bat his blade away, but Edgar deactivated his power in that arm once more, and her forceful swing hit nothing but air. Again, the momentum of her swing threw her off balance and she stumbled down to one knee. She looked up just in time to see the energy blade on Edgar's right hand moving in an uppercut towards her chest. Just as the tip of the blade was about to tear her shirt, Edgar deactivated his powers but continued to follow through with the strike. He curled his hand into a fist and delivered a crushing blow just below Brenda's collarbone. The hit sent Brenda flying backwards. Her powers deactivated as her body was laid flat out with her back on the damp forest floor. She started coughing and curled up into a ball on her left side. As she gasped for air and gripped her chest, Edgar deactivated his powers completely. He walked towards her and bent down on one knee next to her.

"Breathe. Focus on getting air back into your lungs," he said to her. She coughed and sputtered a few more times before finally managing to get one deeper breath that immediately helped. Her chest was still in agony, but she could at least finally start to see the world around her again. And the first thing she noticed was her soldiers pointing their guns at Edgar as they approached from the outer circle. She threw up a hand in their direction, letting them know to stop their advance. They complied.

"H-how?" she was able to say to Edgar between recovery breaths.

"You are strong, Brenda. Hell, if I had met you before this whole adventure started, I don't know if I would've beaten you. But I've been training with a hand-to-hand fighting god for months. If she were here, I bet she would be lecturing you on how large and slow your swings are and how your attack pattern is too predictable. Not to mention that for your whole life, you've mostly tried to avoid drawn-out brawls. But we've all been fighting the most intense battles of our lives for months, getting stronger with every fight."

Brenda was finally able to sit up and perch her arms on her knees.

"The more we fight, the stronger we get?" she asked.

"Yup!" Edgar exclaimed. "When I first met Nadine, I could only activate one blade at a time. I had to choose left or right or neither would work. And if I used my powers, I was exhausted after just a few minutes. And now, well, you know."

Brenda pursed her lips and nodded her head at Edgar. She slowly got to her feet and called the closest soldiers over. After about thirty seconds of discussion, they all turned and began giving orders to everyone else in the camp.

"What did you tell them?" Edgar asked.

"I told them that you are a temporary ally, not an enemy. I told them that our future survival rests on our taking over Quito, that you are here to help us do just that, and that this fight was a demonstration of your ability to do so. And it worked."

Edgar cracked a smile from ear to ear.

"When do we leave?" he asked.

"Right now. I will hitch a ride on your elcycle." Brenda said.

"Great, and if we wrap things up quickly in Quito, what are the chances that I can get you to come back to San Francisco to help us fight Spidre?" Edgar asked.

"Fuck off," Brenda replied.

CHAPTER EIGHTEEN

After barking a few orders to her soldiers, Brenda joined Edgar as he sat propped up against the elcycle, getting food in their bellies and as much rest as possible before the marathon that was about to unfold.

"Do you really think we can do this?" Brenda asked.

"Let me put it this way: I'm more worried about my solo fight in the plant than I am about you and your crew at the headquarters," Edgar replied.

Edgar heard Brenda take a deep breath, he assumed to calm her nerves.

"Do you have any advice since, you know, you've done this 100 times?" Brenda asked.

"It's like five times at most," Edgar replied. "And the only real trick is to keep your eyes open and rely on your speed, not power. We are waaaay faster than normal people, and our energy can easily cut through pretty much anything, including peacekeeper armor and weapons. See who is closest to aiming their weapon at you and hit them before they hit you. Keep doing that over and over until they're all dead or can't fight."

Brenda nodded, and they continued to rest in silence. When Brenda got word that everything was ready, she hopped on the back of Edgar's elcycle as Edgar did his best to program the autonav. It was a tricky route, and he was not a navigation expert, but luckily the route that Symon had entered to get to the powerplant went very close to the military headquarters as well. After a minute of struggle, Edgar got the new waypoint entered and they were off to Quito.

Edgar led the ragtag convoy down the road and in short order the Quito megaskyscrapers broke the horizon line. Soon after, another structure appeared, a huge black dome that Edgar could only assume was the supermassive powerplant. He was certain the long line of vehicles was going to be noticed soon, but it didn't matter. Speed was more important than secrecy for this plan. Everything besides the megaskyscrapers and the powerplant was a blur, and the powerplant appeared larger and larger as Edgar got closer and closer. The autonav took him directly towards the glass front doors of the military headquarters, and he heard the first alarms blare mere seconds before he smashed through and into the main lobby. He and Brenda hopped off and activated their powers as the cycle slid across the floor and barreled through several peacekeepers caught off guard.

"Hit them before they hit you," Brenda muttered to herself as she glanced around. Sure enough, she could tell who among the peacekeepers was closest to firing at her, and she leapt at them with her forearm wrapped in front of her face. She didn't even swing her arm, only the momentum of her jump lent power to her hit, and yet her blade still sliced clean through the peacekeeper's machine gun and deep into their upper chest.

"Jesus Christ," Brenda thought as she pushed the peacekeeper off of her. Edgar was right. These peacekeepers were slow and easy to kill. There was no need for huge powerful movements to break their armor. She saw her next target immediately, another peacekeeper about four feet away about to take aim at her, and she dove for his legs. She slashed clean through his ankles and as he fell, she rose and allowed the back of his neck to fall on her left forearm blades. As his head fell from his body, another peacekeeper with an electric blade charged head-on at her, and she jumped forward from her crouched position, slashing with her right arm through the gut of her newest victim.

Not far away, Edgar was a blur of blue energy amongst a spray of red blood. This was the fighting he loved, the fighting he was practically born to do: close quarters, lots of targets, very few chances for them to get some distance from him or to flee. He cut through any and all light-blue armor that he saw. The few soldiers that attempted to escape out through the main entrance did not meet a much friendlier fate outside, as Brenda's crew was there and ready to mow them down.

After a few minutes of carnage, the lobby had become a bloodstained mess. The peacekeepers who had previously been there were either dead or writhing on the floor in pain.

"Tell your people to come in here and grab any usable guns and armor that they can," Edgar said. "You just keep working your way up until the building is yours. After that, it'll just be a matter of cleaning up any soldiers out on patrol or anyone who I don't take down in the power plant."

Brenda nodded. "Good luck, Edgar," she said.

"You too," he replied, and turned to wrestle his elcycle out from under a pile of peacekeepers. He rode out of the lobby, past Brenda's soldiers, and onward towards the plant. He could hear alarms blaring throughout the city but with his speed, he knew there was little chance of a peacekeeper being able to get a clear shot. As he got closer to the power plant, mounted guns started firing down at him, but the shots trailed way behind. The autonav took Edgar towards one of the access doors and as he was about to crash into it, he swung the elcycle hard to the right. He let go with his left hand, activated his powers, and swung upward through the door as his blade of energy grew to full size. He did a full 360 on the cycle and drove it into the plant through the hole he had just slashed open.

As he drove through the hallway, civilians began opening doors. Edgar finally abandoned the elcycle as people swarmed around him attempting to flee. He turned to the left and started slashing his way through the walls. As he entered a new room, he would run to the next wall and slash through it in the same manner. Over and over, he slashed through walls until he finally made it to his target, a large room with a giant cable in the center. He knew from May's description months earlier that this was the main line that brought power out of the power plant. With one fluid movement, he ran up to the cable and slashed through it entirely while sliding across the floor.

The lights went dim and then out as he completed his slide and turned around to exit through the holes he made. Red emergency lighting came on and he saw peacekeepers running at him through those same gaps. He ran up on them as fast as he could and started slashing. There was little the peacekeepers could do at such close range. Some attempted to aim their guns, others tried to slash with electric blades, but Edgar cut through them all the same. He used his left blade as his primary weapon and stayed close to the still intact left wall that ran all the way back to his elcycle. If any peacekeeper tried to take a wide berth and get around him on the right, only then would he activate the blade on that side and dismember whoever was foolish enough to make the attempt. It was the exact best situation for his fighting style, close combat and only worrying about assailants from one direction.

As he slashed his way forward, he saw that there was only one last big group filing in from another hallway he had slashed through. Seeing this, he focused solely on slashing forward using both blades. Limbs fell and peacekeepers screamed as his blades sliced through everything with reckless abandon. When he made it to the hallway from which the peacekeepers were filing, he kept slashing until there was some distance between him and the nearest soldier, and then jumped to slash at the ceiling above him instead. The ceiling came crumbling down and as his feet hit the ground, he leapt in the direction of his elcycle. The falling debris blocked the hallway, cutting the still-standing peacekeepers off from Edgar and leaving nothing standing between him and escape. He ran for his elcycle, quickly turned it to face the exit, then gunned it out of the building and back in the direction he'd come.

He had done it. The plant was disabled, and now all that was left to do was an incredibly long, fast, grueling ride from Quito to San Francisco. But as he passed the headquarters, he could see that things were not going well. Many of Brenda's soldiers were backed away from the building, firing up at higher floors while peacekeepers fired down at them. Those of Brenda's crew that weren't on the firing line lay dead on the ground.

"*Shit, they were ambushed,*" Edgar thought to himself, and then finally noticed Brenda herself standing in the entryway, just out of view of the peacekeepers above her. She noticed Edgar and stopped screaming orders across the battlefield. She reached out her hand and Edgar grabbed it, swung her onto the elcycle, then gunned his motor to escape without getting shot. When they were safely out of firing range, Edgar came to a stop.

"Ambush?" he asked.

"Those fuckers were waiting for us in the stairwell," Brenda said. "Then when we retreated, they started firing at us from the windows on the third floor."

Edgar thought for a moment.

"So it's only one floor? No shots from anywhere else," he asked.

"I haven't seen shots from anywhere else," Brenda replied.

"Ok, I know what to do," Edgar said.

"What?" Brenda asked.

"You're going to take them all out," Edgar responded.

"What?! How?" Brenda exclaimed.

"Your going to fly up there," Edgar said.

"Fly!? But…"

"Hop on, and be ready to jump off," Edgar said, gesturing to the rear seat on the elcycle. A smile washed over Brenda's face as she realized Edgar's plan. She got on the back of the cycle and Edgar circled around so that he was farther from the building but facing it more head-on. He picked up as much speed as he safely could and when he was just behind the firing line that Brenda's soldiers formed, he whipped the rear of the cycle around. Brenda jumped off at the same time and went hurdling over her crew and towards the gunfire coming from the third floor. The peacekeepers were so focused on firing downwards that they barely even saw Brenda before she barreled through the window and began her onslaught. As the gunfire toward the street stopped, Edgar knew there was little else he could do. He hoped Brenda would finish the fight and was sad he wouldn't see the result or join in the celebration. He turned back towards the path in the autonav, and as the cityscape gave way to jungle, he did his best to put any concern of Brenda's fight out of his mind. He had his own epic battle to focus on.

CHAPTER NINETEEN

FranciscoAs he swung his leg over the remaining elcycle after Edgar departed, Symon looked around at the rest of the group, heading off to different corners of the world, and only one thought came to mind.

What the fuck am I going to do for the next six days?

There is nothing I can do from here to help them disable the power plants, and I can't go to San Francisco yet and risk blowing our hiding spot… I guess I could stay here, I'm sure Rose would be ok with it… but there is nothing to do here by myself? Maybe I could go back to San Diego and see what is left of my hideout? No, that also has a risk of blowing our cover if the patrols are still around…

As Symon thought, his eyes danced around, looking for ideas while scanning the horizon.

What about going to see… no, there is no way… Symon's thoughts continued. *Chicago must still be surrounded by an army and fighting constantly. Hell, there is a chance Spidre already bombed the city to the ground and I would have no idea. And even if he didn't, there is no way I can sneak past whatever siege line they've set up… unless… could that work? There's no way right? Is it worth trying?*

Symon's eyes settled on the horizon towards the east.

The last time we talked, we did suggest that Chicago keep one entry point open to let other refugees in. Maybe they did it and maybe I can get in that way. Well, at the very least, I can burn some time going to check it out. If the plan looks like it won't work, too big of an army or no way to get into the rebel held areas, I'll just come back here and be bored out of my mind for a few days.

With that, Symon programmed the autonav to take him to what looked like an abandoned town about ten miles southeast of Chicago. After several hours of uneventful riding, he made it to an area that was so abandoned nature had almost fully reclaimed it. Not a single building remained standing, and most were just heaps of rock and silt with shrubs growing up through the cracks. After a brief search, Symon found one pile of debris that crumbled in such a way that it made an alcove big enough to hide his elcycle in. He swung the cycle into the alcove and threw his sand-colored tarp over it, making it barely distinguishable from all the rest of the debris. He then began his trudge north, through more abandoned areas towards Chicago's southside.

When Symon had last been in Chicago, days after he and the LO-ECs had annihilated the local regiment that controlled the city and successfully helped the locals hold off a huge counter assault from the world army, the rebel-held area of the city was tiny. It consisted of only a few square miles that had Lake Michigan to its east and the Chicago River to the north and west. Symon figured that those areas would be the hardest to cross. Any bridge that was still spanning the river would have a heavy peacekeeper presence around it, and trying to swim across the river or the lake would run him the risk of getting shot by rebel snipers. He figured his best bet of sneaking in was in the south, where an old crumbling highway marked the border of the rebel-held area. Symon reasoned the heaviest fighting would probably be going on there, and that he could use that chaos to his advantage.

After several more hours of walking, and a couple breaks to eat, Symon finally started hearing gunfire. He continued towards the sounds but stayed close to the abandoned buildings in case he needed to find cover or hide. When he found a building that actually had a still-standing entryway, he ducked into it and opened his backpack. He pulled out the peacekeeper armor with a machine gun attached, which he had been carrying around for months. Normal peacekeeper armor used the soldiers' escaping body heat to power whatever weapon was attached to it, but thanks to the person that Symon was hoping to see now, this armor was customized to use LO-EC-generated energy instead. He slipped his armor piece on and started jogging towards the sounds of gunfire. He proceeded with more caution as the sounds became louder, and eventually he saw his first flash of blue peacekeeper armor as he turned a corner around a building. He jumped backward and pressed himself flat against the building, then slowly peeked his head around the corner. It was two peacekeepers who were facing away from him and towards the southern border of the rebel-held area. He could see that one of them had lines on her armor, indicating she was some sort of commanding officer, and that that officer was holding up her mobile as it displayed a holographic projection of what Symon assumed to be the battle area. The other person looked to be a normal peacekeeper. On his right arm, his armor was equipped with a laser cannon, and his left hand was holding a radio up to his mouth as he relayed orders to someone on the battlefield.

"Oh, perfect!" Symon exclaimed aloud. He turned the corner, aimed his machine gun at the two soldiers, and mowed them both down before they even knew he was there. He walked over to them, grabbed the radio, then ducked back behind the corner he had come from. He removed his armor, put it back in his backpack, and dropped the backpack through a busted-out window of the building. From this point forward, if his plan worked, having a gun would only make things more complicated. He looked the abandoned building up and down to make sure he could identify it and recover his weapon in a few days' time.

"Comms officer down, Officer McDermott now relaying to field!" Symon said into the radio, trying his best to sound nervous.

"10-4. Please relay new orders officer," someone on the other end said.

"New orders passed from command, missile strike inbound, press hard to distract enemy laser cannoneers. Repeat, missile strike inbound, hard press hard press!"

"Fucking finally!" the other person responded. Symon heard the commotion die down, then a much quieter sound of cheers could briefly be heard before the gunfire grew much louder than before. Laser cannon pops and sizzles also joined the cacophony of noise, but then a few minutes later, all went silent. Confident that his trick had worked, Symon started walking towards the southern border with his hands in the air. He eventually was able to see the old highway, which used to be two raised roadways, but the rebels had apparently fully demolished one at some point so that it created an additional physical barrier they could defend. The rebel forces were on the still-standing raised roadway, and all had their guns trained on Symon as he walked forward.

"Halt where you are!" one of them bellowed, and Symon complied.

"Are you military? Are you surrendering!" the same person yelled.

"No and no. Just a man trying to get into the City to see someone!" Symon yelled back.

"You cannot enter, the migrant entrance is a warzone right now. There is a camp set up a few miles to the west, and we will send a team to get you when the entrance is secure!" the person yelled back

"I do not have that time! Please tell your CO that Symon the LO-EC is here, they will know to let me in!" Symon replied.

Even with the considerable distance between them, Symon could hear lots of low murmurs and whispers between the rebel soldiers.

"Come to the rubble pile, we will meet you!" the person eventually yelled. Symon walked forward with his hands still in the air and stopped when he was at the edge of the debris that used to be a roadway. Five soldiers climbed up from the other side and initially kept their guns drawn, but when they saw the metallic holes on Symon's hands, they finally lowered their weapons.

"Glad to see you back, sir," one of the soldiers said. "What brings you here?"

"I came to see May," Symon replied with a big grin.

The soldiers accompanied him under the still-standing roadway, then went up the nearby on-ramp and back to their posts. Meanwhile, Symon clambered up a hill onto the old roads of the city, then made his way to the center of the rebel-controlled area, to the huge megaskyscraper complex that May called home.

CHAPTER TWENTY

Symon eventually found his way to May's building, and as he entered the elevator his heart began to race. A few seconds later, he was hundreds of stories in the air, on May's floor. He found her door, took a deep breath, and knocked.

The door swung open and there stood May. Her grey and black hair was longer than the last time they had seen each other, but other than that and the look of utter shock on her face, she seemed the same.

"You're alone?" May asked.

"I am. Long story," Symon replied.

"How… did any soldiers see you enter the city?" she asked.

"None that are still alive," Symon replied.

"Good," May said as she grabbed Symon at the center of his shirt and pulled him inside. The second the door swung closed, clothes went flying. Things like time, plans, and obligations fell to the wayside. All that mattered to them in those moments was the love they were making.

"Christ, you don't know about much I needed that," May exclaimed as she caught her breath, the both of them finally sufficiently satisfied.

"I think I can relate," Symon replied with a grin.

"I can only imagine the challenges you've had the past few months," May said. "But I would take any of it over what I've had to deal with,"

"And what have you had to deal with?" Symon asked.

"Politics," May replied.

"Say no more. You've had it worse than me," Symon said. May chuckled.

"Don't get me wrong, I prefer what we have now over what we had under Spidre's foot. But the complaining, the manipulation, the power struggle, it's fucking exhausting!" May said.

"I didn't realize you were so involved in the governmental affairs," Symon said.

"I shouldn't be!" May replied. "I'm the best electrical engineer here, and all of our weapons are either pure electric or some level of bio-electric. And we need weapons in good working order to keep the peacekeepers out. So you would think that if I make a recommendation on how to maintain or fix our weapons, people would listen and give me the resources I need. But no! Everyone thinks they know better than the literal expert!"

"Everyone?" Symon asked.

"Well, no, I guess that's a bit overstated." May said. "Some people do listen and make an effort to work together."

"Good. I wasn't ever exactly a politician, but I imagine building a team of allies is a huge help," Symon said.

"Well, yeah, of course it is," May said. "I mean look at you and your team."

"My team?" Symon asked.

"You and the other LO-ECs," May clarified. "You were all

separated from each other, struggling to survive. Then, the second you found each other and united towards a goal, you became unstoppable. I want that same thing, but just for local Chicago politics instead of making the entire world free from terror."

"It sounds like a good plan and a noble goal to me," Symon said, "and I hope you're right about us being unstoppable."

May raised an eyebrow at Symon.

"We're about to try and fight Spidre head on. And everyone besides me is doing exhausting fights and intercontinental trips right before our assault, with no time to rest," Symon explained.

"And you're scared this will finally be too much for you?" May asked.

"I'm fucking terrified," Symon replied. "There is so much that needs to happen for this to be successful. Any one thing that I missed, or any one thing that goes wrong, and we're all dead and the world is doomed."

"But is there another option?" May said.

"No, Spidre kind of forced our hand," Symon said. "It's either go back into hiding forever, take him down now, or die."

"I see," May replied.

"And I know you think we're unstoppable, but we are far from it. There are so many times where we succeeded only by sheer determination, teamwork, and a lot of luck."

"Wait. Are you afraid of dying? Or afraid of failing?" May asked.

"Failing," Symon said without hesitation. "I want this world free from the terror that Spidre created, no matter what."

"Oh, then you have nothing to worry about." May said. Now it was Symon's eyebrow that raised.

"It's like I said before, you have friends, allies," May continued. "It's not just your fellow LO-ECs. There are millions of normal people around the world fighting the same fight as you.”

“But how many of them would actually care enough to stop worrying about their own city and try to fight Spidre head on?” Symon asked.

“I would,” May replied. Symon was floored.

“If I don’t hear from you, don’t see you, and the peacekeepers keep trying to get back into Chicago, then I will know you failed. And the first thing I am going to do is amass whatever kind of army I can and head straight for Spidre’s front door.”

“Holy shit,” was all Symon could say in reply.

“This world deserves peace, and you deserve to be alive,” May said. “If Spidre stops those things from happening, I will come for him, and I know others will, too. And maybe I will fail, too, but the cycle is going to keep going over and over until one day, someone brings him down. So, no matter what, you will succeed, even in death.”

“I… thank you May,” Symon said as he let go a heavy sigh.

“But for the record, I don’t want you to die. I’d really miss the amazing sex we have,” May said with a smirk.

“We’d better make the most of these next few days then, just in case I do die,” Symon replied with a smirk of his own.

CHAPTER TWENTY-ONE

FranciscoNaren and Sera flew high in the air and then to the northwest, taking a wide path around San Francisco out of an abundance of caution. Shortly thereafter, the land gave way to an unending open ocean. They had been in a similar situation once before, flying above the Atlantic on their way to attack the army regiments in Gibraltar. Looking at nothing but blue ocean for that long was exhausting, and now they had to do the exact same thing, but for twice the distance.

"Ahh, I can't take it anymore!" Sera screamed after many hours of holding back.

"I know, I feel like my eyes are going to melt out of my head," Naren replied.

"I have to stop. I have to look at something else, anything else!" Sera said.

"Just hold out a little while longer. Surely, we'll see our rest point soon."

Another agonizing hour passed and finally, something new crept across the horizon.

"The ICT line! Oh, thank fucking Christ!" Sera exclaimed.

The Pacific Ocean was so large that even at full speed, it would take a full 24 hours of flight time. To conserve energy on this trip, they needed a place to stop and rest, and Symon could only think of one location large enough to easily locate in the enormous expanse of water: the Inter-Continental Transit tunnel that connected Hawaii to the rest of the world. The massive tunnel floated at the water's surface, starting at Hawaii in the south and continuing non-stop till it joined up with the main ICT line that ran across the Bering Sea's southern border. From the outside, it was a completely enclosed tunnel with no other land or marker in sight. And just like any other tunnel, a train running through it would have no idea that two people were resting directly above them.

The second Sera and Naren landed, they lay down flat on their backs and started rubbing their eyes. Even with their eyelids shut, the image of sunlight bouncing off of endless waves felt like it had burned into their retinas.

"I don't know if I can handle two more days of this," Sera said.

"Hopefully, after this next fight, we never have to fly over an ocean again," Naren replied.

"I am just going to declare it right now. No matter what happens after this is over, no more cross-ocean flights!"

After another minute or two, they finally opened their eyes and for the first time realized that the sun was setting. They both pulled some food out of their packs and as they ate, a chill started to fill the air. When he finished eating, Naren opened up his backpack and pulled out a tarp and blanket. He laid the tarp down, then he and Sera snuggled in close and wrapped up together in the blanket. As night fell, the only light that could be seen in any direction was starlight and the glow of Sera's skin.

As they sat in the middle of the ocean cuddled up with each

other, Sera suddenly started chuckling quietly.

"What's so funny?" Naren asked.

"My brain is just very weird," Sera replied.

"What do you mean?"

"We're out here in the middle of the Pacific Ocean, in a place where no one has been since the tunnel was constructed. And we're about to go off and do two exhausting battles that might change the course of all of human history. And yet, all I keep thinking about is how badly I want to see Alison and my other followers."

"But I understand, though. They raised and protected you, made you feel relatively safe for twenty years. Craving that before we go into the biggest fights of our lives is understandable."

"I think that's part of it, sure, but there's more. They protected me, but I also haven't seen them since the day we took down the androids. And every time we've tried to go back, something happens that keeps us away for longer. I miss them."

Naren hugged Sera tighter.

"When all of this is over, our next stop is New Orleans. I promise," he whispered. Sera looked up at him and their lips came together for a long, long time. Suddenly, Sera pulled her head back and had had an excited look on her face.

"Do you think anyone has ever had sex here before?" She asked Naren.

"What?!" Naren exclaimed in reply.

"What?" Sera asked in turn.

"What on earth made you think of that?" Naren asked.

"I mean, we were kissing for an awfully long time."

"That's not what I meant."

"You still didn't answer the question," Sera replied.

Naren stayed silent for just a moment.

"No, I doubt anyone has ever had sex here before," he finally replied.

"Think you can spare enough energy to make history in a whole different way?" Sera asked with a smile curling at the side of her mouth. Naren smirked back, finally understanding what Sera was getting at.

CHAPTER TWENTY-TWO

The next day, just as sunlight began brightening the sky, Naren and Sera shared a quick meal, packed up their things, and gazed into each other's eyes as they took to the air.

"Love you," Naren said.

"Love you," Sera replied. With that, they finally parted ways. Naren turned towards the south while Sera began heading northwest.

Compared to the rest of the LO-ECs, Naren had very little time to waste. He was the fastest flyer of the group, but also now faced the longest trip back to San Francisco after the plant in Brisbane was downed. He couldn't attack the plant early to give himself more time to fly back because that could give Spidre's regime a head start on re-routing power to San Francisco. He essentially needed to fly from Brisbane to San Francisco in twenty-four hours with no breaks, so any amount of rest he could get before then was crucial.

How the fuck am I going to do this? he thought to himself. *Even if I can make it to San Francisco in time, I'll be so exhausted from the flight that I'll be useless. I'm already the weakest fighter, now I have to be the most exhausted, too? Hell, do I even have the skills to take down this plant by myself? My weak hits nearly cost us the assault on the net tower, and this time around I won't have Nadine and Edgar around to pick up my slack. I wish there was some way I could do this without fighting so that I'll have more energy in San Fran…*

Naren's train of thought was interrupted by a sudden realization.

Wait a second, I have some time to plan here. I can stake things out and see who is… yes that could work!

Naren spent the rest of his flight ignoring the endless sea beneath him and instead focused on his newly realized plan. Hours passed, and eventually he noticed a large chain of islands. As the islands passed beneath him, on the horizon he saw two huge strips of land.

That's the landmark that Symon said to look out for. I just passed what he called the Solomon Islands, and the two land masses are Papua New Guinea and Australia! Naren started heading for the southern strip of land. As he did this, he also started to descend.

Holy crap, it's just as hot here as it was in the desert, he thought to himself. He carefully surveyed the area. There was not a single sign of human life, be they peacekeeper or otherwise. As he touched down, the fatigue he had been ignoring finally caught up with him.

My legs are wobbly. I need to rest, he thought as he barely kept himself on two feet. He wasn't sure exactly what time of day it was, but it didn't matter. He was exhausted. After forcing himself to stay awake just long enough to eat and unpack a blanket, he curled up on the rocky shore and fell asleep.

When he woke up, it was once again almost sunrise. His body ached from the two straight days of nearly non-stop flight, but he knew he had one more flight to go before he could relax, relatively speaking. He ate another quick meal and then flew into the air as high as he could comfortably go. From what he could see of the shoreline, Naren assumed he was still too far north, and started to follow the coast south and east. He once again followed Symon's guidance and was looking for the first signs of a major population. Brisbane was the furthest city to the north in Australia, so if he kept heading south, he would find it. Once again Symon's geography was accurate. A few hours after Naren had left his campsite, he saw a megaskyscraper complex and a huge black dome.

He landed among a group of old abandoned buildings to take a breather and eat some more.

Ok, time to put this plan into action, he thought.

Naren took back to the air and flew towards the megaskyscrapers. When he finally started seeing signs of life on the cracked streets below, he backtracked a little and then slowly flew around the outskirts of the city. The next two days was more of the same, with frequent breaks to rest and recover whatever strength he could for the long flight to come.

"Finally! A good target," he thought to himself as his eyes trained on the blue uniforms that had wandered away from populated areas. There were four peacekeepers in total. Naren was still quite a distance away, but from what he could see, one soldier was close to his height and body type.

This is the best chance I'm going to get, Naren thought. After one last look around to confirm there were no other peacekeepers, he careened towards the group he had been watching. He plowed into the first peacekeeper, and her body crumpled into the roadway. Naren turned sharply and darted towards the next peacekeeper. He ripped that one off the ground and then aimed directly for the next closest soldier. He scooped them up as well and chucked them both as far as he could. As they came smashing down into abandoned buildings near the road, Naren trained his eyes on the final peacekeeper. He had a laser cannon on his armor but was far too slow to aim it. Naren was on top of him in an instant. He grabbed the soldier by the face and smashed the back of his head into the ground. The officer went limp and Naren took off towards the outskirts again, still holding the now lifeless body by his face.

When Naren felt he was far enough away to land again, he did so and started stripping the peacekeeper down.

Bryant, huh? Naren thought as he looked at the name badge. *I guess I can pull that off.*

Naren tried on the uniform and besides the boots being a little small, everything else fit well enough. He had his costume, now it was just a matter of being a convincing soldier.

He had rehearsed the next part of the plan in his head over and over during his flight over the Pacific, but he would have to wait till the exact right moment to enact it. He lay low and rested as much as he could. An hour before dawn on the day he was supposed to fly back, the time had finally come.

Naren scarfed down the last of his food and left his entire backpack and its contents behind. He couldn't afford to have any extra weight for the flight he was about to attempt. He donned the full armor of the soldier he had killed, tied the shoes to his waist, and took off towards the power plant.

Against the still dark sky, the blue aura coming from Naren's feet was obvious to anyone who looked up, and that was the point. As he passed over more populated areas, alarms started blaring. He continued towards the power plant in a straight line until he heard the sounds of mounted guns taking shots at him. He arced to the right to stay out of range and continued past the plant and into an abandoned building. He quickly threw on the shoes that had been at his waist and rushed down onto the street. When he made it outside, he could clearly hear the commotion of soldiers scrambling from the direction of the megaskyscraper complex. He ran to intercept them and as he rounded a corner was met with the sight of thousands of soldiers rushing from the megaskyscrapers towards the power plant. Without missing a beat, he slid onto the end of one of the lines and started marching along with them. No one seemed to care. Barely even a look of acknowledgement in his direction.

He had done it. He was making his way towards the plant without fighting an entire army. As they got closer to the plant, the street widened and encircled the giant dome structure. Peacekeepers began breaking off to their respective posts and he made his way through them towards the nearest street entrance. He grabbed the door handle and the door sung open.

"Hey, laser cannoneer! You're supposed to be heading for the…" Naren heard some form of commanding officer yelling in his direction, but he ignored it and continued inside. He started sprinting through the building. Occasionally he would see arrows painted on the wall, and he followed the ones that pointed to CONTROL. After some time, he made it to the correct room and walked inside. A half dozen workers at various stations looked up at him in astonishment.

"I have been sent by command to instruct you that the building is under attack. You are to shut down the power as a safety precaution and immediately exit the facility," Naren said, channeling the bold and confident persona that he put on back when he was a military investigator.

"But a shutdown would take several hours to disengage," one worker commented. "Do they understand that…"

"Did you not hear what I just said!?" Naren interrupted. "We are under attack! Command says shut down and evacuate, so shut down and evacuate before a LO-EC fucking annihilates us!"

"Y-Yes sir!" the worker replied, and all six of them began frantically interacting with control panels. After about forty-five seconds, a quiet hum that no one had realized was there started to quiet.

"It's done," a worker said to Naren.

"Good," Naren replied. As the lights in the room began to dim, Naren's shoes evaporated and the light of the blue energy at his feet filled the room. Channeling everything that Nadine had taught him, he used the energy to front flip through the air and bring his heel down through the center of the nearest control panel. The panel splintered into thousands of pieces as the workers frantically ran for the exit.

One by one, Naren did the same flip move through each control panel until only mangled metal surrounded him. When he was sufficiently satisfied that the damage couldn't be repaired in one day, he took to the air and flew out into the winding hallway. He made his way up and left, following signs that took him up to a maintenance exit higher up in the building. He smashed through the exit door and out into the early dawn sky. A few seconds passed before mounted guns started firing in his direction. They were far too late. Naren ripped off his borrowed armor and uniform as he flew and began his mad dash back across the Pacific Ocean.

CHAPTER TWENTY-THREE

When Sera was comfortably far from the ICT line, she flew high into the air to let off a blast. Her power momentarily drained, and she fell back towards the ocean, but before she hit the water, enough power had returned that she was able to continue flying.

I can't believe I have two more days of this, Sera thought, dreading the return flight as she stared at ocean around her.

"I can't believe I have two more days of this!" Sera exclaimed out loud, about five minutes later. "Why should I even worry about the forces in Sapporo or the fight with Spidre, this flight staring at nothing but sun glare and waves is going to kill me first!"

About three hours later, Sera was met with an unexpected surprise. As she flew, the horizon started to grey.

Are… are those storm clouds? she thought to herself. As she flew below them, she started to feel cold drops on her exposed arms and face.

Holy shit, it's raining! Sera thought. She was excited that at least part of her flight was going to have some novelty to it. That excitement changed a short time later, when she saw a lightning strike in the distance.

Oh, fucking hell what are the chances of that! Sera thought. *I get like three lightning storms my whole life in New Orleans, and now I have to fly right through one?!*

Sera tried thinking back to the advice her followers gave her about flying in thunderstorms, but it had been so long it was hard to remember.

Do I fly over it? I vaguely remember someone saying that… no, no, that's not right. They talked about if I should or not but… because of my powers they were worried about lightning going up over the clouds? Or hitting me while I went through the clouds? Maybe? Fuck. No. I don't go over… I go around!"

Sera looked to her left and right and saw storm clouds as far as the horizon allowed in every direction.

"I don't think I can go around this without getting off course, but they said something about that, too… I think if I can't go around, I'm supposed to stay low to the ground… Yeah, that sounds right! So, stay low and hope I don't die. Fuck, that would be such a letdown to die because I got struck by lightning after all we've been through.

Sera stayed as low to the choppy waters as she could and did her best to continue flying straight. This got increasingly difficult as she neared the storm. Wind started howling, and the rain got harder and harder until finally, the sky got so dark it felt like nighttime. Lightning crashed all around her and wind-blown rain hit her face so hard that her eyes stung.

Ok nature, Ok! I get it! I'll stop complaining about the boring ocean! Just chill out already! Sera thought to herself. It had been a long time since she had felt fear like this.

Fortunately for her, the worst of the storm was short-lived. The lightning and heavy rain passed in about 10 minutes, but the wind and some lighter rainfall continued for hours more. She started to shiver at some point, and it only got worse the farther north she flew. She continued to push through it and the rain eventually stopped, but it was still cloudy and cold. After what seemed like an eternity, she finally saw land again. Even better, it was the exact island Symon had told her to look for, a sort of diamond shape but with an arm and hand reaching downward on the western side.

"There's Hokkaido! Oh, thank fucking Christ!" she exclaimed out loud. Sera flew over the island and saw Sapporo right where Symon said it would be, where the arm and the diamond met up with each other.

It was still cloudy and Sera knew her orange glow would stick out against the grey sky. She also wanted to get indoors and warm as fast as possible, so at the first sign of abandoned buildings, she descended. Lots of the old structures were completely leveled. Symon and Naren both mentioned that earthquakes were common here, so unmaintained buildings didn't usually stay erect. In spite of this, Sera found what looked like an abandoned temple or shrine that was still partially standing, and she flew inside.

She opened up her pack and practically inhaled the first food she could find. She then checked the tarp and blanket she had packed to sleep with. The blanket was soaked all the way through, but the tarp was made of a different material that wasn't so easily waterlogged. She shook excess water off, wrapped it around herself, and fell asleep.

Only about two hours passed before Sera was awakened by a commotion coming from outside. She saw lights and heard what she guessed to be several hundred people gathering around the shrine.

"Oh shit!" she said out loud.

She jumped up and was about to crash through the wall to escape, but then heard a word that stopped her dead in her tracks.

"Messiah! Messiah!" the people outside were screaming as

loudly as they possibly could. Sera had heard that word plenty of times before, but never imagined she'd hear it anywhere besides New Orleans. Sera took to the air and gently coasted out of the window she had entered through. As she did so, she looked down at the crowd who all turned to meet her gaze. They all simultaneously let out a gasp, and collapsed to their knees and bowed their heads.

"Messiah, we are overwhelmed with gratitude that you would grace us with your presence!" one person yelled as they continued to kneel.

"Messiah! Today when I saw you descend from the clouds was the happiest moment of my life!" another person bellowed.

"Messiah! We must know! Please tell us what we may do to honor your arrival!"

Sera landed in front of the still kneeling crowd.

"You could stand up for starters. Any does anyone happen to have some dry clothes?" she asked.

CHAPTER TWENTY-FOUR

"How do you know about me? I thought all my followers were in New Orleans," Sera asked. She was flying back down to the group after having briefly left to change into clothes they provided.

"Oh, but Messiah, surely you remember…" one follower began to respond.

"You can just call me Sera," Sera interrupted. "Being addressed by my job description is weird, even if it's something as important to you as a messiah would be."

"Ok, whatever you desire Mes… Sera," the same follower almost seemed pained to address her by name.

"Surely you remember about 18 years ago, when contingencies from our branch and others came to visit you in New Orleans."

As soon as she heard mention of this visit, the memories flooded back to Sera.

"Yes, I do remember!" Sera exclaimed. "Forgive me, I was too young to realize all those new faces were from the complete other side of the world. God, I haven't thought about those days in ages!"

"You mean you didn't come here to see us?" another follower asked.

"Correct, although I am very happy to see you all," Sera replied. "I have been unbelievably homesick lately and even if this wasn't quite what I had in mind, it is still a nice surprise!"

"I am overjoyed to know that we bring you happiness!" the same follower said. "We have of course heard about your pursuits ridding the world of its evils, it is understandable to want a break from that."

The rest of the followers in the large group all nodded in agreement.

"Am I correct to assume you're here to rid Sapporo of its evil-doers as well?" the same follower asked.

"I guess in an indirect way?" Sera replied.

"Is there anything we can do to help?"

"Uh, a place to rest and some more food would go a long way. I have one hell of a fight awaiting me in a few days."

"It would be an honor for us to provide you respite ahead of a major trial."

"What is your name?" Sera asked the person who had been doing most of the talking.

"My name is Avery," they responded.

"It is nice to meet you, Avery. It is nice to meet all of you!" Sera said as she turned to the group.

"Are you the leader here?" Sera asked as she turned back to Avery.

"Yes, Sera, this is my congregation," Avery responded.

"Can we walk together back to wherever you all came from? I think we have a lot to talk about," Sera requested.

"C-Certainly!" Avery responded with a considerable amount of excitement. "Just you and I?"

"The rest of the congregation can come, too, but I would like to talk to you specifically,"

Avery nodded and turned to the other followers.

"The Mes-er, Sera and I will walk together and anyone who wishes to follow, please do so from a few paces back," Avery announced. Many nodded in reply, some whispered quietly to one another. Sera flew up into the shrine to grab the rest of her belongings while the large group shifted around to leave the same way they came.

"So, I do remember that some people came to visit New Orleans when I was very young, but I am very hazy on the details," Sera said. "How many groups like yours are there?"

"It is hard to say now, your popularity has grown exponentially in the last few months," Avery said.

"Exponentially!?" Sera exclaimed in reply.

"Yes. Before you destroyed the Androids in New Orleans, I probably could have counted on one hand the sects that followed you as our savior. There were other sects to be sure, but they were all doubters who thought you to be only an uncommon LO-EC, not a messenger from god. But you have done so much, demonstrated such power, it has become difficult for most to doubt you."

Sera felt bashful blood rushing to her face. Having anyone think she was godly was already odd enough, but for that idea to be gaining popularity made the feeling even stronger.

"I am flattered, really, I am. But there are still some doubters?"

"A few, yes,"

"Are there any doubters within your sect?" Sera asked, garnering a visible look of offense from Avery.

"I'm sorry, that may have been rude!" Sera followed up. "It's just that I am here on a very important secret mission. If anyone here blows my cover, lets the peacekeepers know I'm here…"

"They wouldn't dare!" Avery said with more force than any

other word they had uttered that night.

"I'm glad you're so confident, and I don't want to be rude, but I just met you, Avery. How on earth am I supposed to know if I can trust your confidence?"

"You don't have to. Just kill all of the peacekeepers and then you'll have nothing to worry about," Avery replied. Sera's face jerked up to look in their eyes.

"Well, you are just full of surprises, huh?" Sera said.

"Those are evil people with nothing but bad thoughts rotting their brain. They deserve the kind of peace only you can bring them."

"Jeez," Sera replied.

"This is why we were so excited to see you, Sera. We thought you had finally come to free us from their brutality."

Something about Avery's rage and desperation wasn't sitting right with Sera.

"What have they done to you here?" Sera asked as her heart raced. Her beats per minute went into double time when in response to the question, Avery stopped dead in their tracks and choked back tears.

"Please Sera, I, I'm begging you…" Before the sentence was over Avery dropped to their knees.

"Sera, they are monsters! They do not care about things like military protocol or civilian status. They kill us for the slightest transgression, for the wrong look on a bad day, to let off steam if they don't get paid on time. Whatever excuse they can find to spill our blood, they do it. If there is anyone on this earth that deserves your divine punishment, it is them!"

Sera looked out over the crowd and saw dozens of faces choking back tears, and dozens more all-out bawling. Their pain filled her with a rage she had not felt since she had ripped apart that last android in New Orleans.

"How many regiments police this City?" Sera asked through gritted teeth.

"Only one," Avery replied.

"Do they all live and work and in the same place?"

"There is an operations center not far from the megaskyscraper complex, and a living quarters near the power plant,"

Sera thought for a moment.

"Does either the operations center or the living quarters have an armory?" she asked.

"I think so," Avery replied.

"I need to know for sure."

"Is James here with us!?" Avery turned and yelled to the crowd. A young man came scurrying through the crowd up to them.

"I am honored to be in your presence, messiah. Please let me know how I can assist you," the young man said.

"Call me Sera," Sera replied. "Do you know if the military operations center or their living quarters have an armory?"

"Yes, they both do," James replied.

"How do you know this?"

"I work at the food distribution center for the megaskyscraper complex. Sometimes the military force myself or other co-workers to bring them food in both locations."

Sera thought to herself again for a few moments.

"Do both armories have laser cannons?" she asked.

"Yes," James replied.

"How many?"

"I unfortunately do not know. I am sorry, Sera."

"You don't need to apologize. You've been incredibly helpful already!" Sera replied. James nodded.

"Which location would have more soldiers inside of it right now?" Sera asked.

"The living quarters, for sure," James said.

"Ok. Let me ask you both about the power plant, then. I need to attack it in a few days and bring it offline. With my powers and its safety measures it should be a breeze. But if I'm going to take down a whole military regiment, I can't have the workers sounding alarms and giving any surviving soldiers a chance to radio in the attack."

"Well, you don't have to worry about the civilians working in the plant," Avery said. "The military in charge at the plant are the worst of them all. They treat the regular workers like garbage."

"And how many military are inside the plant?"

"There are 30 soldiers around the outside of the building operating giant mounted guns. Then inside there is a small command unit and some additional officers for relief shifts," James replied.

"Are there at least 90 laser cannons and some machine guns in the armory at the operations center?"

"It has to be more than 90," James replied. "I wish more than nothing else that I could give you an exact number, but it has to be more than 90, and there are definitely machine guns."

"Ok, last question," Sera asked. "Does the Sapporo regiment ever receive visitors or communicate with any other nearby military operations."

"I have never seen another military operation here," Avery said.

"I've never seen one and I've never heard them communicate with others," James said. "I don't think they even can do that right now. They only have those short-range radios, and the closest other regiment is Tokyo, way out of range."

"That is all I need. Avery, prepare your followers, we are attacking the entire military regiment tonight!" Sera exclaimed.

CHAPTER TWENTY-FIVE

"Tonight!?" Avery and James said simultaneously.

"Yes, it cannot wait," Sera replied.

"You have a plan that quickly?" Avery asked.

"I spent my entire life plotting a far more complicated revenge scheme, and then spent months learning from several other brilliant strategists. Yes, I have a plan, and yes it will work, but we have to be careful."

"But it has to be now?" James asked.

"If you want my help, then yes. I have the fight-to-end-all-fights in a few days. I need to recuperate as much strength as I can by then. If we attack right now, I can still have a long rest period while helping you."

Avery and James shared a few rapid-fire glances of excitement and panic with one another.

"C-can you tell us the plan first?" Avery asked.

"Of course!" Sera replied. "We attack the operations center first and attack them hard. It'll be myself and the biggest group you think we can sneak close to the building. I go in first and start leveling soldiers, then your group comes in to pick up their weaponry. At that point, the priority becomes taking down any soldier near an alarm or who is carrying a radio. Word cannot get out about the attack!"

Avery and James nodded.

"We clear out that entire building, not a soul left alive and all alarms destroyed. After this attack, a few people will search the city, killing off any stray soldiers on patrol and disabling any other alarms they seey. Simultaneously, we raid the armory and outfit 90 of your followers with laser cannons and two dozen more with machine guns. They lie low and sneak to the power plant.

When everyone is in position, they attack all at once in groups of three, so three people each firing at one of the thirty mounted gunners around the power plant. When those are down, the machine gunners storm the place and gun down any command or soldiers remaining inside. And while they do this, I head for the military residence and blow it up. All forces gone before day breaks, and with the Net Tower gone the world government will be non-the-wiser. Then I get to relax for a few days before I blow up the supportive suspension of the power plant and then head back to San Francisco."

"Holy shit," James replied when Sera finished. Avery stood with their mouth agape.

"Organize your people, we need to get moving," Sera said. With no further hesitation, James and Avery turned and started barking orders to the rest of the followers. A renewed energy swelled in the group and their pace doubled in speed back to the sect's hideaway. When they made it, Sera was surprised to see it was not much different than the one she had called home for so long. It was still a big room underground that served as a hydroponic garden. The room was a little smaller, but still massive, and the entrance was buried under what looked like a rubble pile but actually had just enough standing walls to keep a crude entrance clear. The most important difference was that this garden seemed to run off of regular power; it did not need Sera's energy or the generator contained inside the torso of a fallen android.

Sera was given some food and some long-sleeved, hooded clothes, so that her glow was less obvious. With a little more planning, the attack party for the operations center was chosen, and they all made their way in small groups towards the megaskyscraper complex. Sera's group darted through the streets and wound up about a block away from the operations center's front door. It looked to be a large, rectangular, single-story building. They waited until it had been exactly an hour since the group left the garden. When the hour mark came, that was Sera's queue to strike.

Sera rounded the corner and rocketed towards the front entrance. Mere moments later, she smashed through the door and as it splintered into a thousand pieces, she surveyed the room. It seemed to be a lobby of some sort, with lots of chairs in the center and a dozen soldiers panicking around the edges of the room. Sera saw one with a radio on his belt and immediately charged. Sera's shoulder buried into the soldier's gut and sent them flying through the wall behind them. The next closest soldier scrambled to pull an alarm that was at shoulder height on the wall, and Sera grabbed the soldier's arm and launched her across the room into another group of peacekeepers. Sera glanced around quickly and didn't immediately see another soldier reaching for an alarm or radio but did see some peacekeepers lifting their arms to aim their guns at her. She took off towards the first and smashed down onto their skull with both fists. Another very nearly got off a shot, but Sera was too quick. By the time the soldier's arm was extended, Sera was around it and throwing an open-hand thrust into the soldier's armored chest. The soldier flew backward from the hit and landed right next to the front door that Sera had splintered.

By this time, the first of Sera's followers were entering the building through that same front entrance, which briefly distracted the soldiers who remained standing. Sera flew in an arc around the room and one by one leveled each soldier with a push or a kick.

"I'm going right, you go left and center. Use the electric swords first and stay quiet for as long as you can," Sera ordered, receiving nods from the now growing group of followers in the room.

Sera flew to the right and smashed through another door. On the other side was a much larger group of soldiers all sitting at long tables, apparently in some sort of common hangout area.

"Perfect," Sera said aloud as her mouth curled into a smirk. The soldiers who reached for their radios were painfully obvious and Sera bounced from one to another with ease, all of them either becoming flattened or thrown across the room into another group of soldiers. Those who were foolish enough to make a run for the alarm on the wall became nothing but an ever-growing pile of crumpled bodies. Eventually some peacekeepers finally wised up and attempted to fight back, but their bullets and blades missed Sera by miles, often hitting other peacekeepers instead. In a matter of moments, what had once been a peaceful rec-room had become a blood-soaked horror. The last three soldiers gave up and attempted to flee, but Sera swung around, grabbed one soldier by his leg, and swung him into the chests of the other two. They all went down. The soldier she had swung attempted to scramble back to his feet, but Sera stomped his skull into the ground and his body went motionless.

One by one, Sera went into any untouched room and, one by

one, any soldier inside it fell. In a matter of fifteen minutes, no soldier could be found still alive.

"We did it!" one follower yelled to Sera as she came back into the first room.

"I did not expect it to be that easy," Sera said. "How did the soldiers in the other rooms not hear us fighting mere feet away?"

"It's because of the building's construction," the same follower replied. "They needed to make it extra sturdy to make it earthquake proof. It's the same for our underground garden. Sturdy materials also block sound."

"Oh, yes, I heard about the earthquakes!" Sera replied. "That's why the power plant has the suspension system too,"

"Yes, that's right! It needed it so that if an earthquake hit, the plant wouldn't get damaged."

"And that's why if the suspension system gets damaged, the plant automatically shuts down."

"Right again. You are a wise woman, messiah."

"Call me Sera."

With the operations center secure, Sera's job from then on became much easier. She watched as her followers raided the armory and started outfitting folks with laser cannons and machine guns. Once the last needed gun and power armor was fitted to a person, other followers led Sera to her next target.

The military residence looked similar to a megaskyscraper, an all-black tower with a black glass facade, but the building was a quarter the typical height. Sera stayed a few blocks away to ensure there was no chance she would be seen. She knew that if an hour passed and no alarms went off, the plan was a success. It would mean that the power plant was surrounded and anyone inside the military residence was none-the-wiser. As the hour mark drew close, Sera quickly ducked down and changed back into one of her special silk kung fu gis that could withstand her explosions. It was still damp from her trip through the thunderstorm.

The hour mark passed without incident. No alarm, no blown cover. Sera took off for the tower and as she crashed through the front door, she unleashed her explosion. The blue churning energy roared out from her body. For just a moment, she could hear the sizzle of the water on her wet gi instantly evaporating. Then the sounds of metal twisting, concrete crumbling, and glass shattering dwarfed all other sound. As she had done several times before, Sera allowed the inertia of her flight to take her through the building and out the other side as it crumbled around her. She skidded across the pavement and into a pile of rubble that used to be another structure. It was well over thirty seconds before the falling building ceased making sounds and started to kick up a massive dust cloud. By then, Sera had recovered enough power to fly and took to the air to look at the scene playing out at the power plant. Just as she expected, a light show was ensuing. Dozens of laser beams lit up the dome and the hundreds of massive hydraulic pistons that made up its supportive suspension system. The laser beams flew up to various parts of the plant as mounted guns fired back in vain. One by one, the guns went silent, and about twenty minutes later, the first follower came out of one of the plant's street level entrance. Sera flew over to them.

"Did we do it!?" she asked.

"We did it!" the follower exclaimed as loudly as they could. Sera jumped in the air with joy, then took off to fly around the exterior of the plant.

"We did it! We did it!" she screamed over and over at anyone in armor that she could see. Eventually, the group all met up with each other and made their way back to the garden as fast as their legs could take them. As Sera entered the garden, Avery was there waiting for her.

"We did it, Avery! Your city and your followers are free!" Sera exclaimed.

Avery burst into tears and ran towards Sera. Sera reached out her arms and Avery hugged her tight.

"I knew it! You truly are sent from god, there is no doubt! No one can doubt!" Avery exclaimed through tears. Sera said nothing, just stayed in the tight embrace and took the moment in.

CHAPTER TWENTY-SIX

As promised, the next couple days for Sera were filled with rest and food, but with an extra side of happiness and gratitude. The night before Sera had to leave, she sat down next to Avery to eat after a long day of talking with her followers.

"Did you have a good day today? I hope that my congregation wasn't so excited that they forgot their manners," Avery asked.

"No, everyone was super nice!" Sera replied. "It was incredible getting to hear everyone's stories. I didn't realize so many people were related to my followers in New Orleans."

"Well, of course!" Avery exclaimed. "Where do you think most of the New Orleans congregation came from?"

"Well, I knew that a lot of them had roots in Hokkaido, I just never realized they were from a different sect that also thought I was the messiah."

"Yes, New Orleans used to be a very small sect. Alison was there with a handful of other local devotees, but that's it. But when we heard of your birth and subsequent miracles, many here moved to New Orleans willingly, and others were asked to go so that we could be ready to serve you when the time came."

"Wait, wait, wait, wait," Sera replied as she shut her eyes and massaged her temple. "Everyone moved to New Orleans solely because of me?"

"Correct. You didn't know this?" Avery asked.

"I didn't, and I don't know how I feel about it," Sera replied.

"Ah, maybe that's why Alison never told you," Avery observed. "She is quite the empath. She must have assumed that you would feel uncomfortable knowing so many people made such a dramatic decision because of you."

"Well, she was right!" Sera exclaimed, taking Avery aback.

"I am sorry if I offended you, Sera," Avery replied, visibly upset. Sera saw their expression and took a deep breath, then exhaled.

"No, I should be apologizing not you," Sera said. "There is a history there you couldn't have known. I just don't understand it, Avery. I get that I'm powerful, I get that I'm unique. And to a certain extent I can understand why now, after everything that's happened, some people might admire me or be inspired by me. But you're talking about people moving across the world to be closer to me twenty-five or twenty-six years ago. Why the fuck were so many people willing to uproot their entire lives for a baby with glowing skin? You have to admit that's weird as hell, right?"

"Well, yes. But faith is kind of a weird thing to begin with," Avery said.

"What do you mean?"

"Well, like you said, you were a baby with glowing skin. For many, that was evidence that you were the messiah. So, before we knew of your existence, what evidence did we have that a messiah was even a possibility?"

Sera stayed quiet, thinking very intently about Avery's question.

"I... I don't know," Sera finally said.

"That's the correct answer," Avery said. "You don't know because there wasn't any. We all believed that a messiah would come to heal our world but had absolutely no evidence or proof of such a thing. We were just a bunch of weird people with a weird feeling about the future; that's all faith is. And that's all we had twenty-six years ago, when we heard about a baby born with glowing skin in New Orleans."

"Ok, that context kind of helps," Sera said. "But if you didn't have any evidence, why did you even think a messiah was coming? And why was my glowing skin evidence that I was it?"

"Well, we may not have had direct evidence till you came along, but we did have some clues. Indirect observations, historical context, patterns that had no other explanation," Avery replied. Sera stared at them blankly.

"Do you know the history of this faith, Sera? Did Alison or someone else ever teach it to you?" Avery asked.

"They tried," Sera said. "It's an offshoot of some much older religion, right?"

"Yes, but that's a bit oversimplified. Our faith is based on ideas that are thousands of years old, but that lost their way over time. Religion started because, for ages, it was the only way people could explain the universe. People could not explain what made the sun rise and set, what made the wind blow, how humanity came to exist. The only explanation they could imagine was that god, some entity with far greater power than us, was controlling it all. And then, to explain why humans still suffered even if a higher power existed, they developed this idea of god eventually granting eternal peace, but only for people who 'deserve' it. For centuries, evil people perverted this idea, used it to manipulate and kill those they didn't like or agree with. And they did this at the exact same time that science started providing real explanations for things that could previously only be attributed to godly power. Eventually, folks got sick of it, and the world rightly abandoned most of what religion had become. All the remained was a small population who had a more figurative belief that some great undiscovered power would lead all of humanity, not a select few, into eternal salvation. Then, when the LO-EC tech was developed and started making its way into the world, many thought it was the 'greater power' we were all waiting for. That belief grew even stronger when babies started to be born with superpowers because of the LO-EC tech. And then, finally, you came along."

"Okay, so…" Sera started to respond but then had to think some more.

"So that explains what led you to believe in the existence of a messiah. It doesn't explain why you believe I, Sera, am it."

"You provide more and more evidence with each passing day!" Avery replied. "First, it was your glowing skin. Then, you manifested the ability to fly. Then, you manifested the ability to project your energy as radiant light. Then, you aided your followers in upgradingthe garden, their safe haven. And then, you started on a journey around the world ridding it of evil and using your radiant energy to do it!"

"No, no, that's not what I am asking," Sera clarified. "Why does glowing skin make me a messiah? Why does fighting Spidre's army make me a messiah? Like, I don't talk to god, I don't feel any connection to a higher power or anything. Why am I a messiah for these things and not just a person with insane powers and a shitload of vengeful bloodlust?"

It was now Avery's turn to stop and think for a moment.

"You would think such a basic question would be easy to

answer," they eventually responded. "I think all of us have a bit of a pre-conceived bias of what a messiah is supposed to look like, and you fit a lot of the description," Avery said.

"There is a description of what the messiah is supposed to look like?!" Sera exclaimed.

"There are a lot of them!" Avery replied.

"How does anyone know what a messiah looks like?!" Sera asked.

"Uhh, they don't actually know," Avery said. "The descriptions are all based on stories that were passed down and shared between different people over hundreds of years. A lot of them are based on real people who existed at one point and who were also thought to be the messiah, but details got changed or exaggerated or ignored over time."

"So, you think I'm the messiah based on what someone else…"

"Oh, wait, I can show you!" Avery exclaimed as they interrupted Sera.

"What?"

"The museum!" Avery continued talking loudly. "There is a painting in there that depicts one idea of what the messiah looked like! I forgot that we could go there now that all the peacekeepers are dead!"

"Someone painted the messiah?" Sera asked.

"Lots of people did all sorts of art depicting the messiah, but it's all old and a lot of it was destroyed over time. But we have one here in Sapporo! Should we go see it?"

"Of course we should!" Sera replied. "Should I fly us there?"

"Of course you should!" Avery replied, prompting a chuckle out of both of them.

Sera and Avery walked out of the underground garden. Then Sera scooped Avery up, and they took off towards the megaskyscrapers. Avery guided Sera to one of the buildings on the northeast corner of the complex and they landed in front of it. There were a lot of regular people outside, and many looked at Sera with unease.

"We're here to go to the museum!" Avery announced, and promptly most people turned back to whatever they had previously been doing. Sera and Avery walked into the building and immediately, Sera realized this tower was unique. The lobby was much taller and wider than normal. It looked like the whole ground floor was one giant open space with various alcoves along the outer walls. Decorative patterns stretched out across most surfaces, and every few feet there was some freestanding work of art or a collection mounted to freestanding pillars or facades.

"This is a… what are they called…" Sera began.

"A public works installation. Yes," Avery replied.

"Yes!" My parents took me to one about a year before… well, everything… I don't know where it was though."

"Do you remember what you saw in it?"

"All I remember is a bunch of really cool old dead animals."

"Probably the natural history exhibit in Atlanta. I haven't been in decades, but I remember it being really amazing . This one is very different from that, though. It is focused on old art from around the world."

"How many of these are there?"

"In the whole world? Quite a few, I think. North America doesn't have many though because the megaskyscrapers are all older versions that were all function, no form."

Sera followed Avery towards the center of the building, where a large elevator bay for the building's residents was located. They continued past it towards a larger alcove near the far-left corner.

There, Sera saw all sorts of beautiful but strange art pieces. There was a giant backlit piece of colored glass that depicted a bunch of people with circles around their heads. There was a green metal statue of a person sitting, dressed in robes and their hair adorned with what looked like dozens of beads. On a small mounted display, there was a drawing of a woman with a lot of arms that looked like it had been torn out of a book.

"There!" Avery said as they pointed past all of it towards a painting so large Sera couldn't believe she'd missed it. It was easily twice as tall as she was. The painting had a bunch of people on a mountaintop, one of whom was a man with long hair. He was at the top of the painting. He looked like he was flying, and a bright white light looked to be emanating from him.

"There, that's the messiah. Or what they thought he looked like over 1000 years ago," Avery said.

"This is 1000 years old!?" Sera exclaimed. Avery nodded.

"Can you see now, the resemblance you bear?"

"I guess? But that's a guy, and his skin is different,"

"Do you think an all-powerful being like god would give any sort of fuck about physical attributes? Of course not! Look at his powers and yours. He flies, he radiates light energy. In this painting, he is allying himself with other messiah-like figures, just like you with your fellow LO-ECs. He is about to rid that little boy on the right of an evil that is possessing him, and the old stories say that after the messiah died, he would return one day to rid the entire world of its evil. He is you Sera, you are him. Anyone who was alive 1000 years ago when this painting was created would say the same!"

The two of them stood there in silence for several minutes, each contemplating the painting in their own way.

"Thank you for this, Avery," Sera finally said. "I still don't feel like a messiah, but I can at least understand why you all feel that way."

"It was my pleasure to share this with you, Sera," Avery replied softly.

With that, they slowly made their way out of the building, stopping every so often to look at some other pieces of art. They flew back to the garden and after a few more hours of relaxation, Sera had to leave. Avery accompanied her to the power plant, walking with her as close as they safely could.

"Are you sure this has to be done? The plant workers are friends to us, they would happily shut it down knowing you needed it," Avery asked.

"I can't risk it," Sera said. "The fate of the world's future rests on this plant not getting power back early. No matter how slim the chance is that someone in the plant messes up, it isn't zero, and zero is what we need."

"I understand," Avery replied with a nod. "I don't know exactly what will happen in San Francisco, but I know that when all of this is over, it will be you that has saved our planet. It is certain!"

"Thank you, Avery. I will never, ever forget you and your congregation," Sera said. They hugged one last time and Sera took off for the easternmost set of hundred-foot-tall hydraulic pistons under the plant. When she was mere feet away, she unleashed an explosion and the pistons erupted into thousands of pieces. The giant structure groaned as its supports collapsed and the plant settled on the rest of its pistons. As the sounds of clanging metal subsided, the plant fell completely silent.

The plan had worked. The plant was down and wouldn't be coming back online until the supports were rebuilt. The second Sera had enough energy to take off again, she did so, and hurdled back towards the Pacific Ocean and San Francisco.

CHAPTER TWENTY-SEVEN

The day had finally come and, as he expected, Symon was the first to arrive at the rendezvous point. He had ditched the elcycle a few miles away and walked the rest of the way to the eastern slope of a mountain that was within striking distance of San Francisco. Even from this far out, it was immediately obvious that the five superpowered LO-ECs had been successful in their assaults. Spidre's compound was normally lit up with the bright orange glow of a force field that could be seen from very far way. Now, all that was there were a series of normal-looking buildings and a dome-shaped central headquarters that looked like a smaller version of the power plants. Atop that structure was a large saucer-shaped emitter, which the force field would usually flow out of.

By now, Spidre had certainly figured out what the LO-ECs were planning and was organizing a defense. On the off chance that scouts were being sent out to look for him, Symon tried to hide as best he could among the rocks and crags of the mountainside. He was more nervous than he could ever remember being, and very much did not want to be the one who messed up the plan. To add to the uneasiness, while it was plain to see that the LO-ECs had successfully disabled the plants, he had no idea whether the five superpowers were injured, or even alive. He breathed a sigh of relief when he finally saw a blue streak of light flying low towards his location. As it got closer, he realized it was Nadine.

Symon popped up from his hiding spot and quickly waved, then ducked back down again. Nadine spotted him and landed about two feet away. The second she touched down, Symon threw some food to her and she gulped it down.

"Everything went smoothly?" he asked.

"It was cold as all hell but otherwise nothing major happened," she replied. "You waited here the whole time?"

Symon shook his head.

"I snuck into Chicago to see May."

"Why did I have a feeling you were going to say that?"

Nadine and Symon only had a few more minutes to share details before they spotted a blur heading in their direction and kicking up a long line of dust and sand in the process. Nadine briefly took off to signal their location, and a few moments later Victor was standing next to them.

"Holy shit, you would not believe the adventure I had," Victor said after catching his breath.

"Are you ok?" Symon asked.

"Yes. My adventure had nothing to do with that," Victor responded through gritted teeth.

"What the fuck are you wearing?" Nadine asked, looking at Victor's unusual purple shirt.

"Oh, this is what fancy people wear, apparently. This part is called a collar," Victor said, pointing at an extra fold of fabric around his neck.

"So, what happened?" Nadine asked. Victor took a deep breath.

"When I arrived in Gibraltar there was a guy named Lenny waiting there for me who knew my name already and asked me to follow him. I choked him for more information but it's ok because later on we were flirting with each other, and I might go try and find him after Spidre is dead. But anyways he worked for a guy named Max who is rich as fuck and weird as fuck. He only hired people whose names ended with 'enny', like Lenny's did. So Max was rich and owned a golden train that only he rode and also owned the power plant and didn't want me to destroy the power plant but brought me there anyway for some stupid fucking reason. Then he threatened me with a bunch of shitty copies of Tank the android but was going to betray Spidre regardless. I didn't trust him, so I destroyed all the androids and the factory that made the androids and power plant and Max's giant house."

As Victor concluded his story, Nadine and Symon stood dumbfounded.

"Uh, wow. There was no way I could've predicted that story," Nadine said.

"Yes… that was… profoundly unexpected," Symon said.

"You didn't have a crazy adventure?" Victor asked Nadine.

"I was just cold…" Nadine replied, then her ears perked up at the faint sound of an electric motor revving.

"Edgar," she said with a breathy sigh of relief. Again, she briefly popped into the sky to show the incoming elcycle where to head. Edgar ditched the elcycle just as the foothills of their mountain began and started to hike up. As he did so, another blue streak circled the sky from the south.

Naren landed where the group was hiding before Edgar got there.

"So, what crazy fight did you get into?" Nadine asked.

"I barely fought at all. I killed a few soldiers, stole one of their uniforms, and pretended to be a soldier to get inside and smash everything without a fight."

"Christ, did everyone have a more interesting adventure than me?!" Nadine exclaimed.

"You, didn't do anything cool?" Naren asked.

"No! I was just cold!"

Edgar then clambered over the rocks and rolled into the hiding spot, which was now getting quite crowded. Nadine ran over and hugged Edgar but then immediately grabbed his arms and straightened up.

"Please tell me your fight at the plant was as boring and routine as mine," Nadine said.

"Uhh, the fight itself was pretty straightforward, yes," Edgar replied.

"Thank Christ," Nadine said.

"But before the fight, when I was riding through the jungle, I met another superpowered LO-EC named Brenda. She is a leader of some sort of guerilla fighting force that lives in the jungle. I helped her invade Quito."

Nadine threw her hands up in frustration.

"Why, what happened to you?" Edgar asked.

"I… was… just… cold," Nadine replied as her eyebrows furrowed.

Another fifteen minutes passed and finally, Sera's orange streak passed by the mountain from the far north. Naren rushed out to greet her and they exchanged a long embrace before heading to the rest of the group.

"Let me guess, you had some amazing, once in a lifetime experience in Sapporo," Nadine said.

"That's an understatement!" Sera replied with glee. Nadine's head sank.

"I met another sect of the religion that thinks I'm sent from god, and helped them annihilate the regiment that violently suppressed them. Why, what did everyone else do?"

"Victor was kidnapped by a rich idiot, Naren pretended to be a soldier and snuck into the plant without a fight, and Edgar met a new superpowered LO-EC," Symon summarized.

"Oh, wow! And Nadine what did you do?" Sera asked.

"She was cold!" everyone screamed in reply at once, startling Sera. Her jump scare and the timing of their uniform response caused everyone to burst out laughing. It was exactly what they needed to relax and be reinvigorated for the fight ahead.

"Ok, we're all here, we all succeeded, and we're all uninjured. Anyone who hasn't eaten should do so now. We have no idea how much longer our window of attack will be," Naren said. Everyone focused up and Symon handed food to those who had not yet eaten.

"The plan is fairly simple to discuss here. I hope it stays that way once we act," Naren continued. "First and foremost, Sera will fly out unencumbered at full speed towards the force field emitter, the big dish on the roof of the largest structure. She'll unleash a blast and disable it. That way if we must retreat, a new attack will be easy to launch. The rest of us will be right behind her. I will carry Edgar and Nadine will carry Symon while Victor stays on the ground. We will drop Symon and Edgar off as close to the main structure as possible; Spidre is almost certainly in there. Edgar will start cutting his way deep into the structure while Symon covers his back and looks out for whatever the secret is that Spidre is hiding. Nadine will stay outside initially to disable heavy artillery, and I'll stay outside to pick off soldiers and be a distraction while Victor air bursts his way through as many soldiers as possible. Once the defenses on the outside are thinned somewhat, Sera will head inside with Victor via the path Edgar carved out. With the two of them fighting Spidre in tandem, and Symon and Edgar dispatching of any other peacekeepers it will be an incredibly tough fight for Spidre, even with his unique powers. Nadine and I will ultimately head inside as well, and we don't leave until Spidre is dead or until the entire compound is devoid of military presence. Are there any questions?"

Everyone stayed silent. The only sounds they could hear were their own hearts pounding in their chests.

"Whatever happens, just know that I love all of you. You are incredible and it has been amazing sharing this fight with you," Sera said.

"Well said," Symon replied. Everyone else nodded.

"So, what are we waiting for? Let's go make history!" Edgar screamed.

CHAPTER TWENTY-EIGHT

Sera flew so fast towards the compound she felt like she might tear the sky. The second she could see the compound clearly, it was obvious that they were ready for a battle. A dozen or so smaller buildings surrounded the giant dome in the center, and all around every building were mounted guns and tanks. Thousands of peacekeepers equipped with laser cannons lined up along the burn marks where the force field used to touch the ground, while other soldiers equipped with machine guns stayed close to the building entrances. Sera shot high into the air and when it looked like she was directly above the emitter, began her dive. She hoped that by coming from that steep angle, the sun's glare would hide her position until it was too late. She was less than 100 feet away from her target by the time alarms sounded. The laser cannoneers and mounted guns turned to fire, but they were too slow. She straightened out at the last minute and as she passed the emitter, let off her blast.

The sound of the explosion echoed and resonated off the dome structure, making an already loud boom into a deafening roar. It was so loud that most peacekeepers couldn't even hear the emitter ripping from its moorings and tearing to pieces. Some parts of the emitter were still quite large, and as they exploded outward and downward, they wiped out dozens of peacekeepers staring up in awe.

Now temporarily powerless, Sera slid to a stop on the roof of the dome and quickly scrambled back upwards. Her explosion had created a considerable dust cloud, which was her best chance for hiding while her energy recovered. Meanwhile, Naren and Nadine were already on their way and carrying Edgar and Symon below them. With everyone distracted by the explosion, they were able to get close before being spotted, and just as the soldiers turned towards them, Victor started going to work. He raced along the desert floor and threw air bursts as soon as he was in range. The laser cannoneers who were closest to him went sailing, as did a mounted gun or two.

Victor continued throwing air bursts non-stop, never giving the laser cannoneers time to breathe and reorganize their defensive line. When a hole was sufficiently opened, Victor veered left and started throwing air bursts at the rest of the laser cannon line, while Edgar and Symon were dropped off about 50 feet from an entrance. Edgar started hacking his way through soldiers while Symon, Nadine, and Naren did their best to keep the surrounding forces distracted. Symon's bullets flew through all-black armor indiscriminately, and Nadine and Naren picked off just enough soldiers to keep everyone's fire aimed at them.

After about ten more seconds, Sera had sufficiently recovered and joined in the aerial assault. Nadine saw some of the fire being diverted away from her and seized the opportunity. She plummeted to earth and landed on the ground behind a mounted machine gun aiming at Sera. Nadine activated her powers and drop-kicked the vehicle, causing it to fly forward several yards and crush more machine gunners in the process. As other soldiers filled the void left by the vehicle, Nadine danced around them, landing blow after blow, leveling soldier after soldier, staying close to her targets to ensure they couldn't get a clear shot. Over the crowd, she saw a tank rotating its main turret in her direction. She boosted into the air and flipped over the soldiers standing between her and the tank, then brought one foot down on the turret. It buckled easily under the force of her blow.

By now, Edgar and Symon had made it to an entryway, and Edgar slashed through the doors. He expected to be met with either an empty hallway with soldiers waiting farther in, or have the place packed to the brim with peacekeepers. Instead, he saw peacekeepers retreating through another doorway at the far end of a long hall.

Are they setting a trap? he thought. Then he realized it didn't matter if they were, the best bet of finding Spidre was to follow those soldiers. He ran forward and Symon followed close behind. With the soldiers outside trying to get away from Symon's onslaught of bullets, Symon was able to turn around and fire over Edgar's shoulder at the door at the other end of the hall. He hoped that doing so would provide Edgar some cover fire. It worked. The soldiers on the other side briefly fired back but then stopped, leaving Edgar plenty of time and space to slash the door down.

Edgar charged into the room with no hesitation and both energy blades out. The room he entered was huge, probably meant for storing large vehicles, but right now it was full of peacekeepers in black armor, each sporting either an electric blade or a machine gun. Edgar knew the gunners had little chance at a clear shot in the packed room, so he stayed low and swung at every soldier he could see with an electric blade. If a soldier started swinging, he cut them off at the pass by cutting their limbs off at the shoulder or elbow. Howls of pain and panic filled the room as more and more soldiers were dismembered by Edgar's relentless assault.

Meanwhile, Symon continued to provide cover fire from the other side of the doorway. The machine gunners on the exterior had a clear shot at him, so he ducked behind the wall and only occasionally poked his arm around to fire more shots. He did hit some peacekeepers doing this, but the main purpose was to keep the forces congregated tightly together around Edgar so he could cut most effectively. After several exhausting minutes of non-stop swinging, the last peacekeepers turned to run for another exit. Symon fired some final shots while Edgar took the opportunity to catch his breath. Symon stepped into the room but then took one surprised step back when Edgar turned to him. He was covered head to toe in blood.

"I need a minute," Edgar said through heavy breaths.

"I don't blame you," Symon replied. "Do you think it's time to call Victor in?"

Edgar nodded as he leaned over and put his hands on his knees.

Symon turned and ran back down to the entrance, shooting at a handful of peacekeepers who had ducked inside for cover.

Outside the building, things were going smoothly. The peacekeepers could not find an answer to Victor's speed and Nadine's combination of agility and strength. Victor had done a full lap around the compound and the laser cannon line was in shambles. And while the machine gunners were distracted with Sera and Naren's dive bombs, Nadine had been turning heavy artillery into immobile hunks of metal.

Symon stood in the doorway and shot only when a peacekeeper

noticed him. He waved up at the three flyers, hoping one of them would notice him. Sera did and knew seeing him meant the next phase of the plan was upon them. She flew in a semicircle around the battlefield to cross paths with Victor.

"It's time!" she yelled at Victor as they passed one another. Victor then did a semicircle of his own towards the entrance Edgar had made, throwing air bursts to clear the way as needed. He and Sera got to the door at the same time and followed Symon back down the hall to Edgar.

"Jeez, this is brutal even for you," Victor said as he took in the carnage that Edgar had created. Edgar shrugged.

The door that most of the fleeing peacekeepers had run towards was to the right of the hallway through which the LO-ECs had entered. The door was still slightly open, so Victor ran forward, pushed it, then ducked out of the way, anticipating gunfire. Instead, it was silent. Sera poked her head through and saw another large room, similar to the one they were currently in. This room was completely empty, but the door all the way across the room was also ajar. The four LO-ECs made their way across the room and, once again, Victor threw the door fully open, then darted out of the way.

This time, bullets rang out as they hit the concrete floor. Symon snuck up to the door and poked his head out, then quickly back in. There were about 30 gunners, all up high and aiming down, and across the room stood an imposing older man with grey hair, a well-manicured beard, and a dark blue uniform with black stripes on the arms.

"Spidre!" Symon yelled as he pulled his head in, and machine guns shot in his general direction. Victor, Sera, and Edgar repositioned further back from the door so they could see in without getting shot at.

"Is that really him?" Sera asked.

"That's him," Edgar said, a shiver shooting up his spine as he remembered their last encounter.

"Holy shit," Victor whispered.

Spidre could easily see the four of them as well and put on a mean scowl as he stared. After several tense moments, Spidre turned and darted through another door and into the next room.

"Shit, we can't let him get away!" Edgar yelled.

"Victor, can you make it across that room without getting shot?" Sera asked.

"I think so, yes," Victor replied.

"Do it. Don't lose sight of him," Sera said.

"But don't engage him unless you have to!" Symon piped up. "Spidre will be a tough fight alone and you've already done so much today…"

"Fucking Christ, Symon, enough! I know what I'm doing, and I'll be fine!" Victor said and immediately darted into the next room. Machine gun fire rang out again, but Victor was too fast. In a flash he was across the room and through the far door.

Outside, Naren and Nadine continued their pop shots at the artillery and soldiers, but the grind was starting to take its toll. They hadn't slept and had taken the longest flights of their lives right before an all-out battle. Nadine flew over to Naren and signaled for them to fly higher.

"We can't keep doing this," Nadine said. "If we're going to have any energy left to fight Spidre, we need to move on."

"Agreed. What do you want to do?"

Nadine dove back down and hovered just out of artillery range above the dome.

"Our fight is with Spidre, not you!" she screamed as loudly

as possible.

"If you want to keep trying to shoot us and wait for your turn to die, then by all means do so! Or you can lay your weapons down and start walking away from here alive! You will not get another chance like this one!"

Nadine wasn't sure if every soldier could hear her, but it looked like enough did for the intended effect to occur. Soldiers started ripping the weaponized parts of their armor off and running away from the dome. As more people did this, more still succumbed to the group influence and abandoned their posts. In a matter of moments, all of the fighting forces outside had turned to flee.

Thank god that worked, Nadine thought, and she and Naren flew towards the open entrance.

Back inside, Symon, Edgar, and Sera were struggling to think up a plan of how to safely get past the gunners in the next room.

"I don't like that he's on his own right now!" Symon exclaimed.

"He'll be fine, Symon, Victor isn't an idiot," Sera said. "Let's think of a plan to take out those gunners and…"

Symon did not let Sera finish. He ran into the room and started firing wildly.

"God damnit!" Sera and Edgar yelled at once. Edgar charged through first and Sera followed right behind. Symon's wild firing made the gunners flinch for a moment, and Symon continued running while firing bullets in every direction. As he made it near the other side, the soldiers regained their composure and fired downward. The volley of bullets landed just in front of Sera, separating her from Symon and Edgar. When the rest of the soldiers took aim as well, Sera was forced to retreat while Symon and Edgar dove forward and through the next door.

"Damnit damnit damnit!" Sera screamed.

"What happened!?" Naren yelled as he and Nadine caught up to her.

"Spidre took off running and Victor is giving chase. Gunners up high in the next room separated me from everyone else."

"Shit," Nadine said.

"We can't slow down now. We fly in at full speed, you go left, Nadine goes right, I go center, and we knock them all down or get shot trying."

Sera nodded and all three of them took to the air. They squeezed through the door and Sera made a hard left while Nadine went right. The three flyers splitting up confused the soldiers enough to delay firing, and by the time they recovered, their bullets trailed behind the LO-ECs' paths. Naren, Nadine, and Sera barreled into the long platform the soldiers were standing on and it buckled. The entire apparatus and soldiers on it fell to the concrete below.

The arched trajectory that Sera took allowed her to fly immediately through the next door while Nadine and Naren had to stop and realign. Sera burst through the door into another empty room. Through another doorway on the far side she could see Edgar standing, facing left, with both blades drawn. Sera flew as fast as she could towards the door. Edgar noticed her at the last second and his eyes went wide. Sera barreled into the room and was immediately flung against the wall by something she couldn't see. The force of the blow stunned her, but she was able to turn and see Victor, with no shirt on, bringing his arm down from having just released an air burst. Sera's eyes instinctively looked right, and she saw an energy blade Spidre had launched mere inches from her.

"No!" Naren entered the room just behind Sera and screamed as the energy blade plunged through the center of Sera's chest and out through her left shoulder blade. Sera crumpled to the floor and the glow of her skin extinguished. Nadine also entered the room and frantically looked around. In the center of the floor, she saw Symon on his side with a gash in his throat and surrounded by an enormous pool of blood. Edgar's electric blades extinguished, and he collapsed to the ground. Despite Edgar being covered in red from his earlier fight, Nadine could see that Edgar was littered with new injuries, though they were superficial compared with what had befallen Sera and Symon.

Naren bellowed with rage and flew head-on towards Victor, who in turn whipped his arm upward and unleashed an air burst directly at Naren. Naren took the full force of the hit and was thrown high into the air. The room they were in now was twice the length of the others they had been in, but the force of Victor's hit was so great that it sent Naren smashing against the far wall very high up near the ceiling. The wall cracked and bowed as Naren buried into it. Spidre took a shot with his energy blades and by a stroke of luck, Naren peeled off the wall at the exact right moment. Spidre's shot pierced the wall where Naren's body had just been, allowing daylight to shine in.

Nadine pushed down her swelling emotions and took a defensive stance. Victor was the first to act and threw an air burst in her direction. Nadine dodged left, hoping that Spidre would think she'd go right; she made the right call. An anticipatory shot by Spidre buried into the concrete. Nadine boosted forward and barrel rolled right at the same time, knowing another burst was on its way. The second air burst flew past her, and Nadine continued towards Victor. Victor attempted a third burst, but it puttered out against the concrete as Nadine grabbed his arm and swung herself down in front of him. Victor tried to bring his other arm around for a punch, but Nadine grabbed that arm as well, and spun Victor so that he was in between Nadine and his apparent new ally.

"Why?" Nadine growled, but Victor didn't answer. He wrenched his arms around and came loose just as Spidre lunged forward with an energy blade protruding from the center of his hand. Nadine activated the energy in all four of her appendages and constantly kept moving. Victor's speed was rough enough to deal with, but one hit from Spidre and it would be all over. With the two of them right on top of her, she couldn't launch a counterattack, only block and dodge. Victor was using every trick in his arsenal, but hits weren't landing. Spidre's powerful blows hurt like hell to block, but at least they were slow. Nadine didn't need to anticipate anything with Spidre. Her reflexes were enough.

As the battle wore on, Nadine's exhaustion was taking its toll. She had to do something to get them off of her. She had no hope of winning the fight, but at least she might be able to get out of there. She dodged to the left after Victor threw a punch, and the move put some distance between her and Spidre. It was her chance. She threw her right arm upwards, hoping to hit Victor's arm and knock him off balance. She made contact, but as she did so, Spidre lunged forward and stabbed Nadine through the lower right ribs. Nadine gasped and collapsed to the ground. Spidre stood over her and Victor stood just behind him, peering over his shoulder. Nadine looked Victor dead in the eyes and his look back at her was completely cold and emotionless, not a hint of sorrow at what he had done.

Nadine felt anger she had suppressed boiling up. Spidre lifted his arm to deliver the final blow, but with one last rage-fueled surge, Nadine activated the jets in her feet and boosted forward into Spidre. As she made contact, she activated the jets in her hands as well, injecting double the force into the blow. Spidre flew backwards and right into Victor. The two of them tumbled away from Nadine, and she knew she this was her only chance. She turned completely around and ripped Edgar off the ground while continuing to fly low towards the back of the room. She had no idea if she could fly while carrying both Edgar and Naren, but she didn't see a point in escaping without at least trying to save the two people who still had a chance to live. She grabbed Naren and swung him onto her right shoulder, then turned to fly towards the sunlight that Spidre had let in when he hit the wall. Nadine was relieved when she was still able to gain altitude, and further relieved when she smashed into the wall and it gave way.

"Follow her!" she heard Spidre yell, and as she ascended she saw Victor head for an exit.

I… have to get high enough that he can't see… what direction I'm going, Nadine thought. She was so exhausted and injured that even thinking was becoming a chore.

Wait, he knows every possible place I could go to hide. Chicago… Edgar's host family… every other city… he knows it all, and with his speed he can… .no… that's not true…

Nadine had a thought and fought with all her might to keep it.

New Orleans… Edgar's elcycle! It has Sera's garden saved in… and Victor doesn't know where…

Nadine was fading fast.

By the mountain… where we met up… Nadine strained to remain conscious as she drifted over to their initial rendezvous point. Whether by luck or by some subconscious memory, she spotted the foothill where Edgar had dismounted. She descended as fast as was safely possible and caught sight of the elcycle on the way down. There was no sign of Victor. He hadn't figured out her plan.

Nadine slung Naren over the body of the cycle, and though her eyes could barely focus, she managed to bring up the autonav and load the coordinates for Sera's garden. She draped Edgar over the handlebars and slid onto the seat, keeping Naren in front of her. She reached forward and grabbed the handlebar, and as the cycle began to move her mind went black.

CHAPTER TWENTY-NINE

Nadine regained consciousness with a start and sat up violently before realizing she was no longer on the elcycle. She was instead lying on a mattress that was placed on top of a waist-high storage crate. She was surrounded by people in a giant room with a very high ceiling. As she relaxed, the pain in her side became immense.

"Lie back down immediately!" barked an older lady with long black hair. Nadine would have done so even if she wasn't ordered to. The pain of her injury was too great to do anything but lie down.

"Damnit, you reopened your wound!" the woman yelled. She beckoned some of the people around her to come help stitch Nadine back up.

"I'm sorry," Nadine said.

"Don't be. I imagine you are in a very different place now from where you were before we lost consciousness."

"Am I in New Orleans?"

"You are. You somehow made it on that loud cycle without the peacekeepers seeing you and all three of you unconscious."

"Thank fucking Christ," Nadine said as she breathed a sigh of relief. At least they were now safe and in caring hands.

"You must be Nadine. I'm Alison," the woman said.

"I know that name well. Thank you for taking us in."

"Without hesitation," Alison replied. Alison continued to work on Nadine for some time but eventually laid down her tools and stood up straight.

"If you are up to it, may I ask you what happened? Naren and your other ally aren't really able to fill in the details," Alison asked.

Up until that moment, Nadine was still in the mode of pressing down her emotions, and instinctively avoided thinking about what had transpired. But when Alison asked that question, the barrier shattered and tears came pouring down Nadine's face.

"If you aren't ready to talk about it that is ok too…"

"We were betrayed," Nadine interrupted and talked as fast as possible to get it all out before choking up. "Our longtime ally joined Spidre and ambushed us and…" she couldn't get the words out.

"Nadine, what happened," Alison said as she stared directly into Nadine's tear-soaked eyes.

"Symon and Sera are dead." Nadine couldn't look at Alison when she said it. She shut her eyes as tightly as she could. Alison gasped and put her hands over her mouth.

"What the hell do you mean?" Nadine heard a voice that she recognized immediately coming from her right, on the other side of the crowd of people.

"Naren!?" she exclaimed, and the crowd of people split. They had been gathered around Edgar, who was still unconscious on another makeshift bed next to her. Past him was Naren, who was awake and sitting upright. It seemed like his entire head was swollen. His face was purple and blue from Victor's blow, his eyes were blood-red from popped vessels.

"You're wrong," Naren said.

"I wish I was," Nadine replied.

"You are!" he screamed. Nadine lowered her head.

"We need to get back there right now and get her out of there!" Naren continued.

"Naren, look at us," Nadine said as she picked her head back up and glanced around. "There is nothing we can do."

"That's easy for you say with Edgar here next to us. If he was in there, would you…"

"Naren!" Alison blurted out.

"It's ok. He's right," Nadine said. "If it was Edgar instead, I would be dragging myself back to San Francisco right now. But that goes both ways, because if it was Edgar, you would be trying to stop me, and you'd be right to do so."

Naren stayed silent and in bed. He lowered his head and brought his hands up to meet his head as he began to sob, the salt stinging his bloodshot eyes.

"How did this happen? How did we not see this coming? How could we let this happen!?" Naren exclaimed. Everyone stayed silent.

"It's not fair. Why did it have to be Sera. Why? Why? era deserved to see a peaceful world more than any of us. Fucking hell, she didn't even get to see her followers again and free New Orleans for them!"

Suddenly, Naren stopped crying. He wiped his tears away, stood up from bed, and turned to face the door.

"Get back to bed! Do you understand how bad of a concussion you have!?" Alison yelled.

"I'm fine," Naren said.

"You're not!" Alison replied.

"Naren, what the fuck are you thinking," Nadine said.

"I'm going to go give Sera what she wanted most," Naren said.

"Naren please!" Nadine pleaded. "You can't fight a regiment by yourself, not like this. They will kill you!"

"Yeah. I think I'd be ok with that," Naren said, and took off through the entryway that he was directly adjacent to. Nadine reached out for him but immediately had to bring her arm back in due to the pain. Her head fell and she sobbed once again.

Naren flew out the door, up through the garden entrance, and hurdled across the sky. His eyes seared with pain as the wind whipped at them, but he pressed through it. He saw the sun to his west and knew that during these hours, most of the regiment would be at headquarters for a shift change. That meant he could skip attacking the megaskyscraper he had called home when he first met Sera. He thought back to that day, and it filled him with rage.

As he tore across the sky, Naren made no attempt to hide his location or plan. He was spotted quickly and alarms blared throughout the city. He paid the alarms no mind and continued directly towards headquarters. As he got close, he could see the main entrance in between old, abandoned buildings. Outside of it, soldiers were lining up to defend. Naren continued at them and when he was in range, they opened fire. Naren rolled to the right and then descended, their shots all following close behind him. As neared them, their shots got closer to him until finally, he ran out of room to roll, and his right arm was torn up by half a dozen bullets.

He did not flinch for a second, and instead used that same arm to ram full speed into the defensive line. Soldiers went flying backwards. Some smashed into the wall of the headquarters, others went through the glass of the main entrance. Naren stayed on the ground and swung freely at anything that moved. His right arm was in agony, but he still threw full-force punches with it and broke clean through peacekeepers' chest plates. He grabbed one soldier under the neck and threw him across his body into some others who were attempting to regroup and fire at him. He leapt into the crowd he had just leveled and pummeled them one by one into the cracked concrete.

While Naren was doing this, some soldiers who had been waiting inside to further defend from the assault rushed out and fired at him. Two bullets hit him in the ribs on his side. Again, he didn't flinch and launched forward. He snatched up all five soldiers who had charged at him and flew with them through the remaining glass door and into the building. He spun and tossed all five of them in different directions, and they knocked down even more soldiers who were lined up in the main lobby of the headquarters. Naren stayed airborne and darted back and forth across the room, smashing everything and everyone in sight. Every chance he got, he rammed head on into a soldier and shoved them through a wall, ceiling, or support beam.

More soldiers rushed into the room from stairwells on either side. Many were still in street clothes but with partial armor on over it, likely troops who had just arrived for the evening shift and weren't yet dressed for duty. Naren boosted into the group of soldiers coming down a stairwell on the far left. He hit so hard that he leveled the entire group and continued forward through the staircase. As he freed himself from collapsing debris, a soldier from within the main room took another shot and hit him in the lower back on his right side. The pain from that one was so intense that he finally had to pause for a second, but quickly his rage escalated further. He switched from taking his anger out on peacekeepers to simply destroying whatever he could. He flew through walls and bashed through support beams.

Bullets continued to whiz past him, and some hit their mark, but he continued smashing everything in front of him. A soldier with an electric blade timed her swing perfectly, and Naren instinctively brought his left arm up to block. The blade cut clean through his ulna, but he fought through the paralysis the electricity doled out and pulled his arm away before it was sliced clean off. The surge of pain from electric shock forced a blood curdling scream from him, and he grabbed the soldier by her face and started flying through walls again, but while holding her out in front. Only when her head had turned to jelly in his hands did he finally let go and continue crashing through the support structures. The building groaned and some soldiers turned to flee, but Naren cut them off from the side and buried the group into the ceiling. The building started to crumble and Naren screamed with rage again as metal and concrete crashed down on top of him. The building fully imploded and buried Naren and all of the soldiers, alive or dead.

As the noises of a falling building subsided and dust filled the air, the debris continued to stir. Naren burst through the rubble but immediately had to land. Multiple bones throughout his body were broken and the building was gone, but he still continued to mercilessly pummel the concrete slabs he stood on. He let out one final scream, but his throat was wrecked from all the dust and previous yelling. His blows to the concrete became weaker and weaker, until finally he could no longer lift his arm.

"It's ok, Sera. New Orleans is finally free," he said out loud in a weak, raspy voice before collapsing on the rubble.

CHAPTER THIRTY

"Holy shit. Holy shit," was all that Edgar could say. It had been two days since Naren had attacked the New Orleans regiment, and Edgar had finally awoken. Nadine had spent the last two days processing what happened and sharing with Alison in mourning.

"So who brought Naren back here?" Edgar said through choked back tears. He glanced over to his right, where Naren was lying down and connected to what seemed like every medical device available in the entire city.

"The congregation did," Nadine responded.

"Congregation?" Edgar asked.

"That's what Sera's followers call themselves."

"Got it. Fuck. How are they handling this?"

"Not well. A lot of denial, a lot more misinformation. People only hearing bits and pieces of the story from others. The only one who seems to have a real handle on everything is Alison."

"I appreciate that, but I think I need to do more," Alison spoke loudly from the far side of Naren's bed.

"What do you mean?" Nadine said.

"I need to get away from Naren's bedside and call a congregation-wide meeting. Get everything out in the open."

"Do it," Nadine said bluntly. Alison was shocked.

"You said yourself, Naren isn't braindead. He's still in there somewhere. If he wanted to die, he would have given up already and done so."

"That's a nice sentiment but it's not how medicine works," Alison replied.

"It's how Naren works. He'll make it a few hours while you handle things. If anything, it might help him to hear your guidance for the congregation."

"That's… a fair point actually," Alison replied after considering it for a moment.

"I want to monitor him for another twelve hours. If he remains stable, I'll call for a meeting and hold it here."

Twelve hours passed, and Naren's status was unchanged. Alison sent messengers to spread word throughout the city of the congregation-wide meeting, and within two hours hundreds of people had piled in through the entrance and past Naren, Edgar, and Nadine on their left. On the other side of the entrance, Alison had set up a crate to stand on while she addressed the crowd. The crowd was so large that they could not fit in the area just past the entryway and had to also line up in the paths that were bisected by hydroponic growth setups. When it seemed like no more people were coming, and everyone had assembled and faced the right direction, Alison stepped onto her crate.

"Tonight, I must forego our usual opening prayers, as a series of events have unfolded that take precedence and must be discussed with full transparency," Alison began, already choking back tears. Some whispers could be heard coming from the crowd in response.

"The rumors you have heard are true. Sera, our messiah, our

beloved shining light, has been extinguished."

The crowd screamed and wailed. Some angrily yelled back at Alison, but their words were incoherent over all the other noise.

"Your anger is understandable!" Alison boomed, silencing the crowd a great deal.

"I am angry! I don't want it to be true! But it is," Alison paused there for a moment to let everyone process her words.

"Sera joined with the other LO-ECs in an all-out assault against the world's ultimate evil. And as triumph came near, they were all senselessly betrayed by one of their own. Sera was ambushed and struck through the heart by a blow that would have turned any of us into dust."

Alison paused again, but this time to compose herself, as tears had come to her eyes once again.

"This revelation has tested my faith more than anything that has ever happened. I expect for many of you, it is a test too tough to bear, and if you want to leave the congregation, I understand."

"If this is true, then how can you possibly stay faithful!? What will god do for us if he won't even save his light?!" one follower screamed.

"I stay faithful because of them!" Alison bellowed, as she pointed over at the three injured LO-ECs.

"Sera was our light, but she was god's messiah, god's messenger. It was her plight that united these LO-ECs, gave them purpose, and led them to create a worldwide rebellion that no army can stop. Given what happened, these three should be dead, too, but they are still here for a purpose. The fight isn't over, but Sera's part in it is. She fulfilled her duties and has moved on from this world. Now, it is up to us to provide healing hands, so that these three can lead the world into its new age."

The congregation stayed silent.

"I do not expect anyone to make a decision here and now. Take the information I have provided and do what is best for you. If I must care for this garden and these three warriors myself, then so be it."

Nadine and Edgar stared out at the now silent crowd. Suddenly, Edgar's eyes were drawn to movement on his left side.

"He moved!" Edgar screamed. Alison, Nadine, and the entire congregation looked at him.

"Naren, Naren moved just now!" Edgar yelled. Everyone intently looked at Naren and after a few seconds, they saw him roll his head left, then right, then settle in the middle again. Alison smiled.

"Pray for their strength, everyone. Whether you believe or not, they are our best chance at a world rid of evil. You may stay or go as you please," Alison concluded.

Many left while some stayed and asked Alison various things. Some asked for spiritual guidance, others immediately asked what they could do to help. When she had finished talking with her congregation, she walked in between Edgar and Nadine and beckoned them to lean in as close as possible.

"I hope you do not mind, but I need to speak low. I do not want the rest of the congregation to hear this," Alison said. Edgar and Nadine nodded.

"Alison, the leader of this congregation, has a heart filled with faith and love, and wants you to be healthy so you can bring peace to this world. Alison, the adoptive mother of Sera, has a heart filled with rage and bitterness, and wants you to be healthy for revenge."

Alison's sudden change of tone made Edgar and Nadine's heart race.

"Kill them. Kill them both and rip their compound to the ground. Make them suffer for what they have done to my sweet little girl burdened with greatness."

For the first time in days, Nadine felt some strength and focus return to her.

"I promise, Alison. When we are healed, they will die."

CHAPTER THIRTY-ONE

"Let's go over it one more time," Nadine said.

"Ahh!" Edgar screamed in frustration. "We've been over this a million times already. Why do we have to go over it again?"

"Because either I missed something or you're leaving something out."

It had been two days since Alison's speech, and while Naren was still unconscious, Nadine and Edgar had made some healing progress. They were now able to walk a little, but currently they were sitting in their beds, facing each other, and obviously frustrated.

"You did miss something. We all did," Edgar said. "Victor is a traitor, thought up this whole plan with Spidre, and everything else was him leading us on. That's it."

"It's not! That doesn't make any sense!"

"Why not!?"

"So you think that over twenty years ago, Spidre went up to an eight-year-old and said, 'go hide in the woods for two decades until you happen to see an android getting attacked by some people you don't know, then lead them on for months of fighting, kill tens of thousands of my soldiers to do it, destroy my irreplaceable net tower and power network, and bring down my one-of-a-kind protective force field that has kept me safe for decades, so that you and I can then reveal at the last minute it was all a ruse to kill them?' You think that conversation with an eight-year-old happened?"

"No, that would be ridiculous," Edgar replied.

"Thank you!" Nadine said.

"I don't think he was hiding in the woods for twenty years," Edgar continued.

"Ugh!"

"Spidre got word of Naren's plan somehow and sent Victor there a few days before to set up the camp,"

"That's even more ridiculous than your idea of Spidre recruiting a child."

"That wasn't my idea, that was your guess at my idea."

"You were in Victor's camp! Did that look like a camp that had been set up for a few days?"

"I actually don't know. I think that's the only camp I've ever been in."

"Victor had dried meat from dead animals hanging in the trees. He had a shelter with marks in the floor from him sleeping in the same spot for twenty years. His clothes were so thin and tattered that they barely covered him. Plus, he had been stealing food from transport vehicles the entire time he was living out there, and that fact was independently verified by Naren and Sera. Do you think they were in on the ruse too?!"

Edgar thought for a moment.

"No, probably not," he finally admitted.

"Good. Now please, go through everything again," Nadine said through gritted teeth. Edgar let out a big sigh and then took a deep breath in.

"The last time I spoke to Victor was outside of the room where the gunners were all up on that high landing. We saw Spidre walk out of that room and didn't want to lose him. We asked Victor if he could make it through without getting shot, and he was confident he could, so he went for it and made it."

"Who asked him if he could make it?" Nadine asked.

"Sera did," Edgar replied.

"Did Symon have any input?"

"He told Victor not to fight Spidre alone and was worried about how much Victor had fought already."

"Of course he was…" Nadine said.

"Hey, could that have been the reason? Maybe Victor was just sick and tired of being held back by Symon?"

"That logic would only explain Victor attacking Symon, and maybe Naren since he also gave Victor a hard time sometimes. It wouldn't explain Sera. She was Victor's best friend. They shared some very deep, personal stories and she helped him work through a whole host of emotional issues. It just doesn't fit."

"Damn," Edgar replied.

"Please keep going, Edgar. There is something in this story, I know there is."

"So, Victor ran for it and made it through the room easily. Sera, Symon, and I tried working out a plan to also get through, and eventually Symon panicked and just started shooting into the room."

"That seems out of character for Symon, but I guess it was a unique situation. And he cares about Victor's safety a whole lot. And he had no way of knowing we were about to come in with more aerial support."

Edgar shrugged.

"It seemed like the best call to me, I just wish he had given us a heads up so we could've planned our run better," Edgar said. "The split second of a difference is what separated Sera from us."

"So, Symon runs across the room while firing everywhere, you two follow, and when the soldiers started firing again, they drove Sera back?" Nadine asked.

"Sort of? More like we dove forward to avoid the bullets and she jumped backwards."

"Ok, so now you're in the room with Spidre and Victor. What happens?"

"Spidre is to the far left, Victor is to the right. I thought they were in the middle of a long-distance fight or something, cause Victor's shirt was torn off."

"That's right, he was shirtless. Why the fuck was he shirtless?"

"It was definitely torn or cut off if that helps any. I saw it near the door at one point."

Nadine lowered her head and started massaging her temples.

"Ok, keep going," she said.

"So, I saw Victor raising his hand to do an air burst and I assumed he was aiming at Spidre, and I think Symon thought the same thing. But instead, he fired it at Symon. The blow sent Symon flying, and as Symon flew towards Spidre, Spidre shot off his energy blade and hit Symon in the throat."

They both paused there for a moment to choke back some tears.

"Keep going," Nadine said quietly.

"When… when Symon went down, I just went into full defense mode. I dodged their ranged attacks and I guess that got Victor frustrated because he ran towards me and started throwing punches. Spidre charged in too, and dodging their close-range attacks was much harder. I tried, I really did."

"I know."

"They wore me down and landed a lot of hits. If they had kept going, they would have definitely gotten a fatal blow soon, but when they heard the commotion you three were causing in the other room, they both backed up."

"So, they definitely had a plan to ambush the three of us."

"Definitely. My memory starts getting hazy there. I do think I remember seeing Sera coming towards the door, but too fast for me to warn her. That must have been around when I collapsed."

"Did you ever see them talk?" Nadine asked.

Edgar thought about it for a few moments.

"I think so. I think Spidre told Victor to back up when they heard you all fighting in the next room."

"So, Victor actually followed a direct order from Spidre?"

"Yes, unless I completely hallucinated it because of my injuries."

Nadine rubbed her temples again and let out a loud grunt.

"I need to get up and walk around, think all of this through. You want to join me?" Nadine asked.

"Absofuckinglutely," Edgar replied. The two of them slowly slid out of bed, and Edgar offered his hand to Nadine for balance. She took it, and together they started limping around the perimeter of the garden.

"So, you're sure you saw Victor's torn shirt on the floor? Nadine asked.

"Positive. It was that weird purple shirt the rich idiot gave him. There was no mistaking it."

"If that's true, then they must have at least fought briefly before you and Symon got there. But then when you were there, Victor wasn't just getting some sort of weird retribution at Symon for giving him a hard time. He was actively taking orders from Spidre. How the fuck could he have changed his mind that quickly?"

Edgar thought about it for a few seconds.

"What if Spidre blackmailed him? Or gave him some amazing offer that Victor couldn't say no to?" Edgar hypothesized.

"What could Spidre possibly offer him?"

"Sparing his life?"

"Victor knew he had the upper hand in the fight."

"Money? Power?"

"Victor doesn't give a shit about either of those things."

"Hmm. Maybe Victor's parents are alive and Spidre is holding them hostage? Wouldn't let them go unless Victor betrayed us?"

Nadine thought about that theory for some time.

"It's the best idea so far, but still is just too convenient. It assumes that Victor would just believe Spidre. Victor was initially distrusting of most people he met, and understandably so. That would be doubly so or more for someone with Spidre's reputation. Even if Spidre had some hard evidence to show Victor, it's tough to imagine him completely joining Spidre's side in a matter of a couple minutes."

Edgar sighed.

"So, we still don't have any good idea," he said. "Actually, I don't think I have heard an actual idea out of you yet, it's all been me."

"I just don't know what to think. Your theories are helping, though, so keep them coming."

"They're helping you figure things out?"

"Yes. You're really helping me think all the evidence through. I feel like the answer is staring us right in the face, but it just hasn't clicked yet."

As they spoke, they started nearing the first corner of the perimeter. There, following the wall itself wasn't possible, because a makeshift fence had been put up around a metal, grey, oval shaped object with dozens of wires running out of it.

"I have been meaning to ask, what is that?" Edgar asked Nadine.

"I honestly have no idea," Nadine responded. They walked up to the fence and stared at it.

"I feel like I've seen this before somewhere…" Nadine said.

"Hey! Hey you over there! Can I ask you a question?!" Edgar yelled to someone who was tending to crops down one of the rows. The person set down their tools and jogged over.

"Are you all right?" the worker asked.

"Yes, and I'm sorry to interrupt you over something so silly. I was just wondering what this thing is?" Edgar asked.

The worker cocked his head to the side, seemingly confused.

"I feel like if anyone should know what that is, it'd be you two…" he said.

"I agree. It's honestly annoying me that I can't figure it out," Nadine said.

"It's the torso of the android Sera destroyed. It powers our garden now," the worker responded.

"Russ! That's why it looked familiar!" Nadine said. "We actually never encountered Russ, only his bigger counterpart Tank. This just looks like Tank's torso but smaller and less armor."

"About one year on and it's still humming along and growing our food," the worker said. "One small gift among many that our beloved light gave to us."

"Thank you for the info. Sorry again for interrupting your work," Edgar said.

"No trouble at all," the worker said, and went back to his row. Nadine and Edgar continued to stare at the torso.

"It's so strange to think that this thing is the reason all of us met," Nadine said. "Had it not been for Sera wanting to rip this thing apart, we would have never known each other existed."

"Yea. Same thing goes for if Symon hadn't invented it in the first place," Edgar said.

"Yeah, that's a fair point… wait a sec… Symon… yes, he invented this… he invented…" Nadine suddenly became lost in thought.

"What the hell are you…"

"Shh, shut up for a second!" Nadine interrupted Edgar. She let go of Edgar's hand, sat cross-legged on the ground, held her head with both hands and stared at the floor.

"Symon… invented this… and the armor… and… what the fuck was it?"

"Oh, like an energy reducer or something?" Edgar said.

"Yes! I bet that's it! Edgar, you fucking genius!" Nadine exclaimed.

"What do you mean that's it? What the fuck are you…"

"Alison! Alison! Alis-ow!" Nadine interrupted Edgar again but, in her excitement, she jumped up too quickly and pain radiated from her side. Alison came sprinting over from the other side of the garden.

"I told you to take it easy and this is what…"

"Save the lecture. I need your help with something much more important," Nadine interrupted again. "Do you know anything about LO-EC anatomy?"

"I mean, my messiah was a LO-EC, so yea I tried to read up as best I could," Alison replied.

"Does the LO-EC system ever cross over with our brain?" Nadine asked.

"Of course it does! You don't have to be a LO-EC expert to know that!"

"But is it just a little bit or…"

"They are inseparable!" Alison replied. "The LO-EC device gets implanted, then grows a conduit network that siphons away body heat to the microtransformers that convert it to usable energy. The conduit network grows wherever it has room, mostly next to veins, arteries, and larger parts of the nervous system. All of those go directly to the brain. I assume it's even more connected in a superpowered LO-EC such as yourself."

"So, if someone invented like a mind control device, it could make it to the brain through the LO-EC conduits?" Nadine asked.

"I mean, sure. But if you're talking about science fiction like that, the possibilities are endless," Alison said.

"It's not science fiction," Nadine replied. "Symon, the other person Victor and Spidre killed, invented a device over twenty years ago that was supposed to be used to turn off LO-EC power. It would have had to reach the entire body to do that, right?"

"Yes, to guarantee it didn't keep siphoning away energy in a dangerous way," Alison said.

"And it would have needed to be quick and easy to administer if Symon was intending to use it on such a large population," Nadine continued. "Spidre would have had that tech and would have had twenty years and the best scientists and engineers besides Symon to figure out how to turn it into a mind-control device."

"That was the secret!" Edgar exclaimed, finally catching on to Nadine's idea.

"Exactly!"

"What does that mean?" Alison asked.

"When Sera's revenge plot against the androids was put into action, both she and I were captured by two different captains. She was captured by the androids, and I was captured by Captain Byron. Both had reputations for being unrepentant ruthless killers.

But instead of killing us, Sera and I were sent on transports to San Francisco."

"Wait, I thought the androids did that because Naren made up a clever lie to that same effect," Alison said.

"He did tell the androids that lie, but they also got orders from Spidre to do exactly that. Spidre wanted LO-ECs alive, and we never figured out why. And now, Victor out of nowhere betrays us, but only after fighting Spidre first, and had his shirt ripped off so Spidre could easily get at the microtransformer on Victor's chest."

"Holy shit," Edgar and Alison said at the same time.

"We didn't see Victor's betrayal coming because neither did Victor!" Nadine exclaimed. "He is as much a victim in this as all of us! And we need to get healthy and get the fuck back to San Francisco to get our friend back!"

CHAPTER THIRTY-TWO

It had been four days since Symon left, and since May had not heard anything, she feared the worst-case scenario had come to pass. She had shed a few tears during quiet times, such as the one she found herself in now, cooking a meal in her apartment. The politics of a local Chicago that was still in the midst of rebellion had become a welcome distraction, and she forced herself to think about that instead. It made it even more shocking when, out of nowhere, there was a knock at the door.

She sprinted across the room and flung the door open and was surprised when it was not Symon waiting for her there.

"Victor, hi!" she said. "Where are the rest of the LO-ECs?"

"I am looking for them now. Have you seen them?" Victor replied, as he stood in the doorway in a newly acquired military-issued black button-down shirt.

"What do you mean? Aren't you supposed to be with them?" May asked,

"No. So they aren't here?" Victor asked.

"No. They aren't. What is going on?" she asked in response.

"Ok, thanks," was all Victor answered. He turned towards the emergency access stairwell.

"Wait, you aren't going to answer me?!" May asked.

"I can't. I have two more places to search, and then I have to go tell Spidre what I found."

"Wait, what the fuck does that mean!?" May screamed, but Victor ignored her and sprinted into and down the emergency stairwell. He was very relieved that it was wide and he could see a landing or two ahead. He was worried it would be as cramped as the dreaded elevators.

Victor continued running after he left the stairwell and when he got to the river, he jumped as far as he could. The inertia of his run carried him over the river, and he picked up his pace again as soon as he landed. He didn't stop until he was in the desert, in the center of the town Edgar's host family had sheltered them in. He wolfed down some military-issue preserved food and then got to work.

I don't think checking door to door is the right strategy here, he thought, and commenced throwing air bursts at every structure he could see.

What a fucking idiot, Victor thought to himself as buildings burst open around him.

What a stupid order for him to give, 'search every location you've ever visited. Find them and kill them'. They aren't here, of course they aren't. They know that I know where this place is, so they won't go here. How the fuck does Spidre not realize that? Does he think Nadine is an idiot? She's in New Orleans or some other place I've never been. Maybe I just shouldn't listen and go to New Orleans anyway.

Suddenly, a thought occurred to him that stopped his barrage of air bursts.

"Wait, why the fuck am I listening to his orders in the first place? Wasn't he our enemy? But… now he's not… Whatever, he's the one I have to listen to now so I guess I will, but it's still a stupid fucking order.

Victor went back to throwing air bursts until every single building was leveled. The thought crossed his mind that he should have checked the tunnels, but the idea still filled him with dread. And besides, Spidre told him to check places he had visited, and technically he had never visited the tunnels. He was only shown where their entrances were.

Well, that's done with. One more place to check.

Victor had started his pursuit of the still living LO-ECs in Monaco, the farthest location they had visited together. He then worked his way backwards through Gibralter, Halifax, New York, Pittsburgh, his old camp in Louisiana, then Chicago and now the desert town. There was only one more location to check, Symon's old hideout in San Diego.

Since the city had been completely leveled by bombs at some point, Victor doubted he would ever find the old hideout. His order was to check every location they had ever visited, but how would he know when he had found it if the whole place was an ashen wasteland?

Ok, let's think about this. How do I narrow down this stupid search that will lead nowhere? he thought to himself as he stood atop the same hill all the LO-ECs had gathered around just a couple months prior. *I remember it being past a lot of old smaller buildings. We didn't pass any big buildings and there were no big buildings nearby. It was all those little house things. So, if I follow that road we first entered by, and stay away from the areas where giant building debris is, maybe that will narrow things down?*

He found the highway they all used to get into San Diego back when they first met and followed it to an area that didn't have large piles of metal and concrete.

Is this area right? Fucking hell, I don't know.

He started to look among the debris piles but did not see

anything that distinguished one from another.

How the fuck am I going to do this!? There is nothing to see here but burnt wood and tiny rocks! What could I possibly find that… oh, wait… the hideout itself! It was a basement and Symon said basements were rare here! If they're rare, maybe they were hard to build, so harder to destroy?"

Victor shrugged.

That's basically the only lead I have. Let me try looking for a basement that survived being bombed and if that doesn't work then I don't know what the fuck to do.

Victor's realization about the basement turned out to be crucial. After an hour of sprinting back and forth over the area, he found a pile of rubble with a mangled basement entrance at the back of it. The whole area surrounding it was barren, but the entrance looked to be in decent shape compared to the surroundings. He ripped the metal doors off and, sure enough, there was the hideout. He sprinted inside and, as he suspected, no one was there.

Wow, it survived! he thought to himself. Besides a coating of dust, everything was as they'd left it. The dental equipment, the cooking appliances, even the mattress on the floor with all the chairs facing it. Seeing this place that was full of good memories sent a wave of happiness over him for the first time in a while.

"Man, I didn't realize I missed this place so much. It was so much fun hanging out here with everyone, laughing, getting stronger, learning stuff. It's too bad I need to kill them all."

Victor's happy feelings were immediately gone.

"That's right. I killed Sera and Symon. Oh fuck, why the fuck did I need to do that?!"

Victor fell to the ground and sobbed uncontrollably.

"They were my friends! Why did I need to kill them if they were my friends?! And why the fuck do I have to hunt down Nadine, Naren, and

Edgar!? I don't understand why! Why!?"

"Why!?" Victor exclaimed out loud.

"Why?! Why why why why why why why why why?!"

Victor curled up into a ball and sobbed for a few more minutes, but as he did so the emotions slowly subsided.

No. It's ok, he thought to himself. *I follow Spidre's commands, that's all I need to understand. Everything will be ok as long as I follow Spidre's commands. Its ok that I killed them because Spidre said to do it.*

He nodded his head to reassure himself.

Well, they aren't here, so I guess I don't need to destroy this place, he thought, and promptly left to run back to San Francisco. When he got there, he ate more military-food rations and then made his way through the wide but winding halls of the main building's upper floors. He had only been there once before, immediately after Nadine escaped, and wasn't sure he would remember the way. After one or two missteps, Victor eventually found the right hall and at the end of it was Spidre's main office. As he got closer, he could hear angry shouting from the other side of the closed door.

"Unacceptable! Three months is unacceptable!" he could hear clearly. The response was quieter, Victor couldn't hear it through the big doors and thick walls.

"Well, go back and tell the engineers their plan is shit and to make a new one. I need my force field back now!" he heard Spidre again.

Victor pushed the door open and everyone turned to look at him.

"We are bus— oh, it's you," Spidre began to shout before realizing who had entered. Spidre motioned for Victor to step further in, the rest of Spidre's personnel gazed at Victor with unabashed contempt.

"Provide us an immediate debriefing," Spidre barked at Victor. Victor remained silent.

"Sir, remember that orders need to be concise and understood for the implant to work," a subordinate said. "Ask for specific things, and in such a manner that this simpleton will understand you."

"Right," Spidre responded with a groan. "Please tell me and the other people here what actions you took since we last spoke and if any of the escaped LO-ECs were found and killed."

"I searched every location we visited as a group," Victor responded. "I started at the farthest east in Monaco and worked my way west all the way to San Diego. I did not find any of my fellow LO-ECs."

"Did you and the other LO-ECs ever agree on a different location to retreat to if your plan did not work?"

"We never discussed it," Victor replied.

"Ugh. Fine. Do you know of any other LO-EC allies that your group met who they may be hiding with?" Spidre asked, again, not realizing that the way he phrased the question kept him from answers Victor had. Victor suspected they were in New Orleans, but there were no other LO-ECs there.

"I only know of two other LO-EC groups besides ours. One is an ally; the other I am not sure."

"Why aren't you sure?"

"I never met them. I only heard a very vague story from Edgar about them."

"Do you have any information as to their location?"

"Somewhere in the jungle south of here."

"Great, they're hiding in the fucking jungle now. Where is the definite ally group?"

"In Halifax."

"You will go there tomorrow and see if your LO-EC friends are there—"

"Wait," Victor said as he interrupted Spidre. Everyone jumped when it happened.

"How dare you give me an order!" Spidre hollered. "You are to respond to only my commands and nothing else!"

"I will not find my friends in Halifax. I checked there yesterday," Victor continued.

"Go anyway. Kill any LO-EC that you can find. And do not dare interrupt me again!" Spidre shouted. Being unexpectedly interrupted had clearly shaken him.

"Understood," Victor responded.

"You are dismissed," Spidre said. Victor continued to stand in the same spot.

Spidre groaned again and rested the bridge of his nose between his fingers.

"You can leave this room now," Spidre said, and Victor immediately turned towards the door.

The next morning, Victor grabbed more military rations and left the compound to sprint across North America. The trip was long, but uneventful. He made it to Halifax after sunset and stopped right outside the rebellion-held sector to catch his breath and eat. He then walked up to the debris pile that marked the border wall. Locals donning military armor popped up and pointed their weapons at him.

"Stop! What is your business here?"

"I need to find and kill the LO-ECs," Victor replied.

"You're not fucking getting them unless every last one of us is dead!" a local screamed back.

His phrasing was very unfortunate.

"Oh, ok," Victor replied as he threw up both hands and two air bursts rocketed towards the defensive line. Locals screamed as the debris pile and all who occupied it were suddenly airborne. Victor sprinted through the hole he had made as others on different sections of the makeshift wall opened fire. Their bullets were far too slow. Victor darted up the side of the debris pile and when he reached the top, was arm's length from the closest local. Victor thrust his palm deep into their chest, then with his other hand threw an air burst down the row through all the remaining fighters on that side. Victor whipped around to his left to throw another airburst across the hole he had made before darting back down the rubble pile and into the center of the rebel-controlled section.

"I wonder if 'every last one of us' means I have to kill all the rebel fighters, or everyone in the city," Victor thought to himself. *"Well, I guess I'll start with the fighters and then cross that next bridge when I have to… oh wait, maybe he meant I only had to kill everyone that was on the wall for defense? I'll go over to the megaskyscraper and find out."*

From his prior recent stop in Halifax, Victor knew exactly what building and floor the surviving LO-ECs lived on, and he dashed through the city towards its location. When he arrived, he looked the building up and down one time before noticing some rebel fighters rushing out of the nearest other building. Victor ran towards them and threw an air burst that flung all of them back towards the doors they had just exited.

"Retreat! Regroup!" he heard some form of commander yell from inside the doors. Victor turned his focus back to the first building.

There is no way they're still in their apartments with everything happening, Victor thought. *I guess the easiest way to kill them is to destroy the whole building. But am I even able to bring this whole thing down?* He immediately brought both of his arms over his head, then down to his side at full force. A massive air burst flung forward and ripped through the building's windowed exterior. The sounds of shattering glass, wrenching metal, and terrified screams filled the air, but the building remained standing.

Damn, it's too sturdy. I'm not going to be able to stick in one place long enough to destroy it, he thought, and began to run around the building, throwing air bursts at it as he did so. More screams, more shattering, more wrenching. When he had finished one loop, every exterior facing window on the first twenty floors was gone.

Victor ran into the building and began looking over everybody he could see. The LO-ECs would be easy to find, since they'd be the only ones with metallic holes in their hands. One by one, floor by floor, apartment by apartment, body by body he searched, but to no avail.

I guess that makes sense, Victor thought. *They're the most powerful fighters in the city. They're probably out holding a defensive line somewhere.*

Victor ran back down the same staircase he had used when he first entered the building. He knew that by now, the locals would have had enough time to set up a counter-offensive outside. Sure enough, the second his head poked out into the lobby and was visible to the street, dozens of shots rang out. Victor jumped back into the stairwell for cover and then ran back up a few flights for good measure.

Ok, so it looks like I at least have to kill those locals outside, not just the folks who were defending the wall, Victor thought. He ran up another five flights and then exited the stairwell. He barged into an apartment, ran up to the window, and before the rebels could train their sights on him Victor's airburst was already on its way. It careened into the center of the group and the fighters scattered, be it through their own power or Victor's. With their offense shattered, Victor sprinted back downstairs and unleashed hell.

Locals were fleeing in every direction, and Victor couldn't let them escape. He threw air bursts at the farthest targets from him, then started chasing down those that were close by. He caught up with the first, pulled them to the ground by the back of their neck, then stomped full force on their chest. He saw the next-closest fighter frantically turn to take a shot at him, and he lunged forward and landed a palm thrust square on her chin. Her neck snapped back violently, and she collapsed to the ground. The next closest person was not even looking back at the carnage as he fled, but Victor caught up to him all the same. As he did so, Victor swung outward with his left arm and landed a violent shot directly to the fighter's temple. The fighter was sent reeling across the ground and finally came to rest in a lifeless pile thirty feet away.

Victor repeated this over and over, one by one, methodically ending every armed fighter he could see. Then, suddenly, a thought occurred to him:

I wonder if I should ask one of these people how many of them I have to kill before I can find the LO-ECs. Maybe they know!

Victor found his next target and instead of immediately going for a fatal blow, he grabbed the man by his head and pinned him to the ground.

"Please! Please have mercy!" the local pleaded.

"I just need to know how many of you I need to kill before I can find the LO-ECs," Victor replied.

"Wh-What does that mean!?" the fighter yelled out. Victor let go of the man's head and picked him up by the shoulders instead.

"Listen," Victor began to explain. "I'm not a monster, ok? I don't want to kill people if I don't have to. The guy on the wall said I have to kill all of you before I can find the LO-ECs and kill them. What did he mean by…"

Victor was interrupted by his own reflexes. At the top of

his peripheral vision, just above the head of the local he was interrogating, he saw a bright green pinpoint of light that his brain immediately recognized as a threat. He dropped the local fighter and jumped back as a laser cannon beam from a mounted gun buried into the dirt where he had been standing. He looked up and saw the cannon jutting out of a window high up in a megaskyscraper, way out of range of his air burst. He could see it was being readied to fire again. Another shot came out and Victor dodged it. Another shot, another dodge. And another and another. After a few more dodged shots, Victor noticed some locals just starting to peek their heads out from behind cover.

Damn it, I don't want to get pinned down here," he thought. He danced around shots for another second to figure out what floor he needed, then he darted into the building and towards the stairwell. He smashed through the stairway door and on the other side was a winding staircase with at least two dozen locals pointing their guns at him.

Trap! Victor thought. The fighters all jumped with a start when Victor sent the door flying, and that half-second delay kept Victor from being completely riddled. Victor's reflexes kicked in and he threw an air burst up the stairwell, but not before a few bullets were fired off in his direction. One hit its mark and buried deep into the meaty part of his right thigh. He ignored the pain and jumped backwards out of the stairwell as pieces of it came crashing down. When the commotion had silenced somewhat, he poked his head back in and saw that most of the bottom two levels of stairs had collapsed, and the locals that ambushed him were either dead or too preoccupied with their own injuries to care about him. He looked around and the closest functional staircase was in front of him between the second and third stories.

If I get a running start and jump from the top of this rubble pile, I might make it. But my fucking leg, he thought. He lightly grabbed his throbbing thigh.

He considered his options and swallowed hard. He sprinted over to the elevator, and it opened upon sensing him waiting there. Victor looked inside for less than a second and already the walls felt like they were closing in on him.

Fuck. Definitely not an option, he thought as he backed away to keep his head from spinning. He looked back towards the staircase, shook his head to give himself a mini psych-up, then ran for it. His thigh ached, but he took off with the uninjured leg, stretched above his head as far as his arms could go, and managed to grab hold to the bottom support of the landing. He swung himself up and over and continued without further obstacle to the floor where the laser cannon had fired from. He knew it was possible that during the time he was held up in the stairwell, the cannon had been turned around to shoot at him as he entered whatever room it was in. So, as he got to the correct floor, he slowed down and inched the door open. He poked his head through the crack and saw a completely empty hallway that split in multiple directions. He silently followed the right-most path towards the side of the building he had entered from. And when he made the last turn, he sprinted forward and tried to make as much noise as possible doing so. He sprinted all the way down the hallway and heard a laser cannon blast open a door behind him.

Figured it out! he thought as he turned and saw a splintered door blown from its frame. This time, he had been the one to trick his foe. He now knew what apartment to attack. He sprinted for the wide open hole and leapt through it. Another laser beam sailed over the length of his body as he dove forward. Victor's inertia carried him across the entirety of the small apartmentand directly into the mount for the cannon. The cannon lurched forward and tumbled out of the shattered window it had been firing from just a couple minutes prior. Victor landed on his left side and saw what could only be the cannoneer swinging an electric blade down towards him. He rolled out of the way and swung himself back to his feet. It was then that he finally noticed who the cannoneer was.

"Victor!? What the fuck are you doing!?" Will screamed. He was standing tall and had light blue peacekeeper armor on his right arm that extended into an electric blade. The blade had extra wires running out of it that were connected to Will's palm.

Oh, cool, the blade is being powered by his LO-EC energy! Victor thought.

"Hi, Will. I need to kill you," Victor responded.

"Why the fuck are you doing this!? Why do you want to kill me?!" Will continued to yell.

Victor thought for a moment. "I don't think I actually want to kill you. I just have to," he said.

"Fuck you!" Will screamed and charged at Victor. He jabbed with his electric blade with a quick flick of the wrist. It was a weak strike, but incredibly quick and still had the full might of the electric blade behind it. There were maybe five people on earth who would have been able to dodge such an attack, and unfortunately for Will, Victor was one of them. Victor swung his body to the right out of the way of the blow, then reached past the blade to rip Will's armor off. But Will continued lunging forward and threw his arm up and out just as Victor was grabbing hold. It was a remarkable parry that sent Victor reeling on the balls of his feet. Will did not let up. He kept charging forward and taking small flick-of-the-wrist jabs at Victor.

"Holy shit he's good," Victor thought as he recovered his balance. This was the kind of opponent Nadine had warned him about

ages ago. Will was slower and weaker but understood fighting mechanics well enough to give Victor trouble in spite of it. A combatant like him was the exact reason Nadine wanted to train Victor on proper fighting technique. Victor attempted to dart right and get some distance for an air burst, but Will saw it coming and moved to counter. A single step to the left and another quick attack from the wrist was all it took to force Victor to dodge and lose all his momentum.

At this point, Victor was on the verge of being cornered and had to change strategies. He squared up with his hands in front of his face just as he had practiced with Nadine. Will came at him with another jab, and Victor leaned out of the way. Another jab, and another lean in the opposite direction. On the third jab, Victor tried to get around and inside to the right of the blade, but Will saw it coming and moved ever so slightly to keep the electric blade between him and Victor. Victor reset back to his squared-up position and Will came at him again. Victor leaned to his right again and Will went to block again, but this time Victor's move was a fake-out. The second Will went to block, Victor went left around his blade and grabbed hold of Will's forearm from below. He sank his fingers into the armor and wrenched Will's arm downward. Will cried out in pain as the electricity in the blade sparked out. The force of Victor pulling downward caused Will to step forward and line up perfectly with a left hook from Victor directly to the ribs on his exposed left side.

Will fell to one knee and spit out globs of blood as he coughed and gasped.

"Will, I need to know how many people I need to kill before I can find the other LO-ECs. Do you know?" Victor asked.

Will continued to gasp and cough up blood.

"It doesn't matter… how many people… you kill… they won't tell you…I won't tell you… You will never find… my LO-EC brethren."

Contrary to the fighter on top of the rubble pile earlier, Will's wording was very fortunate.

"Oh, thanks. So, I'll only kill you then," Victor replied, and brought his right fist down hard on the back of Will's neck. An audible snap rang out and Will fell flat to the floor. Victor took a deep breath, and sprinted back down the stairway, jumped to the ground floor, and then ran out of the building and out of Halifax.

CHAPTER THIRTY-THREE

Edgar repositioned his feet with an energy blade extended and swung his right arm around toward Nadine as she charged. The switch-up in his stance would have fooled most fighters and left them wide open for a blow. Unfortunately for Edgar, his foe was not like most fighters. Edgar's swing was just wide enough that Nadine adjusted and thrust her left arm upward with the full extension of her body. Edgar's swing stopped coming and instead his arm was thrown up towards the sky. Nadine planted her other fist into the center of Edgar's chest but held back considerably on the force of the impact. Edgar took a single step back and let out the slightest grunt. He had lost the sparring match, but this wasn't about who won, it was about testing if their wounds had healed.

"You're good?" Nadine asked, Edgar nodded.

"You?" Edgar asked in kind. Nadine also nodded. If she still had any lingering injury, her block of Edgar's blow would have certainly made it apparent, but she felt fine.

Edgar withdrew his energy blades and moved his arms slightly upward and outward. Nadine ran into his arms, and they embraced.

"We're back," Edgar said softly.

"Thank Christ. This was the longest ten days of my life." Nadine replied.

"But now is the hard part. What are we going to do about Spidre and Victor?" Edgar asked. They both remained silent and embracing each other. They stayed in that position for well over a minute, only breaking the silence when Alison walked over.

"He's moving a lot more, but still out," Alison said as she neared. Nadine buried her head in Edgar's chest.

"Even if he was awake, he would be in no shape to fight, right?" Edgar asked.

"Absolutely not," Alison replied. "With those wounds, we're looking at months of recovery, even for folks like you."

"So, it's probably better that he's still asleep, right? I mean if he was awake, he would either want to come fight, or try to stop us from going," Edgar said.

"I'm not sure he's wrong in the latter case," Nadine replied.

"What do you mean?" Edgar said.

"We can't wait for Naren to recover, not without risking Victor either finding us or Spidre using him for some fresh new hell of a plan. But there is no reliable way for just us two to beat Victor and Spidre either. Spidre is physically the strongest of us, Victor the fastest by a mile, and they both have ranged attacks that lessen my one advantage of being able to go airborne."

"Well, if there is no chance of winning why did we push so hard to heal and—"

"I didn't say it was no chance," Nadine interrupted and finally ended their embrace. "You and I are experienced fighters with lethal one-hit power. If we happen to catch Victor off-guard immediately and down him, then the two of us together could probably take down Spidre. But that is a big 'if', and only works if Victor is the first to go down and we completely abandon an attempt to reason with him or knock him out.”

“You don’t think we could beat Victor even together?” Edgar asked.

“It’s the same situation, we get that one hit in it’s all over, but he has such a versatile arsenal to keep that from happening. Because of our training he is at least on-par with me if we engage in hand-to-hand combat. But he can disengage at any point and with too much speed to counter it. If he stays right out of our attack range and keeps throwing air bursts, it’s only a matter of time before he wins.”

“So maybe we try to sneak attack?”

“They would be somewhere within the giant compound. Spidre spent twenty years inside of that thing, they won’t be leaving anytime soon. So, to sneak up on Victor, we would have to sneak into the compound and find the room they’re in while going completely undetected.”

“Maybe we split up? Do you think one of us could take on Spidre alone while the other distracts Victor, then we double team?”

“I mean, we’re definitely stronger than the last time we fought Spidre. I think there is a chance either of us could take Spidre down alone, but it’s not a guarantee. And then we’d still have the problem of a double-team against Victor also not being a guarantee. Ideally, I’d like to go in with something with a higher chance of success.”

“Maybe there is some way to get Victor back on our side first? Either cut the mind control thing out of him or just convince him to stop?”

“I would love to get him back that way, but I just don’t see it happening. I’d be willing to bet that the mind control thing is in the microtranformer on his chest. That’s his only microtansformer. If we cut it out of him, he would eventually die like he almost did in Monaco. That didn't look like a peaceful way to go. And if we try to convince him to stop fighting us, we'd have to do it in the middle of him fighting us."

"Well, if there is no hope of saving him, maybe we just keep fighting him until he overloads on power again?"

"We have little way to know when that will happen. Even if his twitching is increased from when we last saw him, it could be a few minutes or a few weeks till he overloads."

"Damn. Could we recruit some help? The LO-ECs in Halifax? Some of the Chicago forces?"

"They both have their own fights to worry about, and with Victor's air bursts, our numbers advantage could dwindle immediately."

"Maybe we just engage both of them in close hand-to-hand at the same time? Like, all four of us just in there together all frantically trying to land hits?

That idea made Nadine stop and think.

"Best idea so far, but still a problem if Victor decides to disengage with us. He has the speed to get out of there and start a brand-new assault.

"God, Victor is so tough to figure out. The more we talk the more I'm scared to fight him over Spidre," Edgar said.

"Me too!" Nadine said. "Spidre hits hard but his accuracy with his ranged attack isn't the best, and if we do engage hand-to-hand it's much harder for him to back out to try a different strategy. He also doesn't know all of my tricks, fades, and fake-out moves. Victor does."

They paused again, but Edgar broke the silence fairly quickly.

"Victor doesn't know all of my moves, though," he said.

"What do you mean?" Nadine asked.

"I mean I didn't spar with Victor nearly as often or as intensely as you did. He can predict you but might have a tougher time with me."

Nadine paused again, this time for much longer.

"You might be the better person to fight Victor between the two of us," she finally said. "And conversely, I'm probably the better person to fight Spidre. But your lethal blows are on the slower side, and they're close-range only."

"That's… not entirely true," Edgar replied, causing Nadine's eyes to go wide.

"What the fuck does that mean?" she asked.

"There was something Symon said ages ago, about why my power is different from Spidre's. I bet if we…"

"There is no fucking chance we're letting that plan happen," Nadine said as she caught on to Edgar's plan.

"Why?" Edgar asked.

"Because you would probably die!" Nadine exclaimed.

"But there is no way he'd see it coming. If you're looking for a higher-odds successful plan, that's the one," Edgar said.

But… I don't want to lose you," Nadine said, as she leaned in for another embrace with Edgar.

"I don't want to lose you either. But in all these scenarios there is a chance that one or both of us won't make it. That doesn't change with this new plan, but there is a good chance Victor will die too. After that it's just a matter of you bringing Spidre down."

Nadine sniffled as she stifled back tears.

"So we engage in close combat with both of them at once and try to keep it that way. We go for lethal blows while also trying to snap Victor out of the effect of the mind control. And if you get hit…"

"Then I bring Victor down with me and it becomes a one-on-one between you and Spidre," Edgar said. Nadine nodded softly.

They ate some food and tried to sleep as best they could, but their nerves were fried. They instead spent most of the night cuddled up with one another, hoping it wasn't the last time they would do so.

They said their goodbyes to Alison just before dawn and started their journey west. They took turns manning the elcycle to conserve energy. It was an uneventful but anxiety-ridden journey, as both of them thought in silence about the two possibilities that lay ahead: their demise or being the direct cause of death to one of their best friends. It was late afternoon when they made it to their final rest point, just before the compound came into view over the horizon. They ate and embraced one last time with tears in their eyes.

"Whatever happens, just know that I will always love you," Edgar said quietly.

"I love you, too," Nadine replied. As they let go of each other, they wiped the tears from their eyes and their expressions turned serious. It was time to focus. They got back on the road and immediately noticed something wasn't right. The compound took much longer than expected to peek over the horizon, and when it did they were met with a jagged pile of rubble instead of the giant dome. As they got closer, they could see that the entire compound, the dome, the surrounding buildings, everything, had been leveled. It looked like the place had been bombed in the same way San Diego had, only without all the scorch marks and ash. The sight made Nadine and Edgar shiver. When they made it within the borders of the compound, they found the largest pile of rubble where the dome used to be. In front of it were the bodies of all the engineers, mangled and twisted from injuries they had sustained. And at the very front of the heap was a large, headless body they could not mistake.

"Holy shit," Edgar finally blurted out. As they got closer, a hint of black sitting on the rubble pile caught their eye. It was Victor. He was alive, but he had scabbed-over injuries all over his body, and his twitching had gotten much worse since the last time they saw him.

"Victor, what the fuck happened here?" Nadine asked.

CHAPTER THIRTY-FOUR

"Report!" Spidre barked at his lead engineer.

"Sir!" the engineer replied. "There were a few unexpected results, but ultimately the trial was not successful, as we assumed would be the case."

Spidre grimaced.

"You had them in the KROE this whole time?" he asked.

"Yes, sir. As soon as you brought the two of them down here, they went straight into the KROE and we fired it up."

"Fine. What were your unexpected results?"

"There were many. For both participants, their LO-EC system was putting out energy readings the entire time they were in the KROE. We did not expect any readings from dead participants. The readings were small, barely detectable, even with our equipment, but they were there. Their injuries also seemed to have gotten smaller. This normally wouldn't be a big deal; I would expect injuries like those to grow or shrink depending on how the body began to break down. But their bodies never started the breakdown process."

"What do you mean?" Spidre asked.

"I mean they never entered rigor mortis or showed any of the other early signs of decomposition. But they are dead, no pulse and no brain activity."

"Theories?"

"I mean, we've never studied subjects like these before. No one has. The only time we had a similar situation in the past was in very different circumstances that called for our work to go a different way. So, this could be completely normal for a dead superpowered LO-EC and we wouldn't know."

"Only one of the subjects was superpowered," Spidre replied.

"So that is the last unexpected result. Despite both subjects being dead, the KROE seemed to try to do its job anyway. The regular LO-EC's energy conduit system changed completely, despite the subject being dead."

That revelation made Spidre very nervous.

"And the superpowered one? Any change?"

"Inconclusive. Their conduit system was already overly complicated and intricate. It is hard to tell what difference, if any, the KROE made. If you want, we can continue to do some other tests and—"

"No, no more tests, I've heard enough," Spidre interrupted. "The last thing I need is one of those corpses continually storing power and then one day randomly creating an explosion like that woman could. Bring them down to the lower level for cremation immediately. When you have completed that task, bring our controlled LO-EC up here. It is time."

"Yes, sir," the lead engineer responded with obvious disappointment. The engineer gave directions to his team, and they manipulated control panels that were connected to a seven-foot-tall, three-foot-wide metal cylinder mounted and isolated from everything else on the far wall. The door of the cylinder swung open, and the bodies of Symon and Sera came tumbling out. Spidre went to his office while the engineers loaded the bodies onto wheeled motorized tables to assist in bringing them downstairs.

A few hours later, the lead engineer came up to Spidre's office to get him.

"It is done?" Spidre asked. The engineer nodded.

"And the controlled LO-EC is in the lab waiting for you."

"Good."

Spidre made his way through the halls to the lab, where Victor stood waiting.

"I have questions to ask you before I give you your next task, since I am not fully confident you will live through it," Spidre said.

"Ok," Victor replied.

"Do you know, or have any idea, what that is?" Spidre, asked, pointing at the cylinder Sera and Symon had been in.

"No," Victor replied.

"Sir, that question may be too vague. You need to be specific and detailed," the lead engineer said.

Spidre groaned again.

"Dealing with this mind control is exhausting!" Spidre bellowed.

"It is a learned skill, it will get easier," the engineer replied.

"How specific do I need to be?"

"The more details, the better. He should be able to listen and confirm what he knows when you've finished."

"Fine," Spidre said as he turned back to Victor.

"I am going to monologue, and you are going to listen. You will tell me what, if anything, is familiar to you from what I have said. Do you understand?" Spidre asked.

"Yes," Victor replied.

"Good. Over twenty years ago, the LO-EC extermination movement was sparked largely by one event: when a superpowered LO-EC blew up a non-LO-EC sector in the city of Boston."

"I am familiar. Symon told us about this," Victor said.

"Most of the world believes that the person responsible for this attack was never found. In reality, he was found and exterminated immediately. He had not intended to blow up anyone. The power had built up in his body over his life, and he just happened to be in the wrong place when it finally released."

"I am familiar with the first half of that. Symon told us the person was never identified and the motivation was never known," Victor said.

"I saw the writing on the wall even in those first moments, that this attack meant the end of the world's LO-EC population," Spidre continued. "And as a LO-EC responsible for the LO-EC extermination, I knew any number of people might come to kill me, so I wanted to become stronger. I enlisted the top engineers I could find to develop a way to give me more power, and this dead superpowered LO-EC ultimately provided the key."

Spidre motioned to one of the engineers who turned to his control panel and entered a few commands. The cylinder on the wall began to rotate, exposing the rear section that had previously been within the wall. On the back panel behind some form of clear vacuum-tight paneling was the body of a male in his late teens. His skin was pale blue, his head was thrown completely back with his mouth wide open, and dozens of wires were connected all over his body that ran out to different parts of the cylinder. Victor's eyes went wide, and his breathing quickened at the sight of the monstrosity in front of him.

"I-I am not familiar with this," Victor eventually sputtered out.

"Why does he keep doing that?" Spidre asked.

"Doing what?" the lead engineer replied.

"Interrupting me," Spidre said.

"Oh, you didn't provide a specific time when he should respond regarding his familiarity with your information."

"I swear to god I fucking hate this mind control thing," Spidre responded, and turned to Victor.

"When I finish speaking completely, I will let you know. At that point you will respond and tell me what, if anything, you are familiar with of what I said. Do you understand?"

"Yes."

"Good. I am actually surprised that Symon didn't know about this. Actually, I bet he did and just didn't tell you, that sounds more like the Symon I know. This apparatus was built by another engineering team, but was based on a lot of the groundbreaking work in LO-EC-energy-based healing that Symon had been working on.

This device is the KROE, the Kinetic Reorganizer of Organic Energy. When a participating LO-EC user enters the device, the KROE uses the superpowered individual's unique and complex LO-EC system to force the participants LO-EC system to grow. It can turn a normal LO-EC user into a superpowered one, and did so for me twenty years ago. And I believe it can turn an already superpowered LO-EC into a god. Of course, I also thought it might be able to bring a dead LO-EC back to life given the work Symon had been conducting, but evidently that is not the case.

You see, this was my big secret, why I wanted one of you alive. This, along with the little trick with Symon's energy suppressor, are my key to holding power over this world. It has been over twenty years since the LO-EC war, and people have forgotten how dangerous you all are. I wanted to give them the reminder to end all reminders; a superpowered LO-EC with unbelievable power, terrorizing the globe, bringing deaths by the millions, who would ultimately be felled by my regime. But in reality, that terror would have been under my control the whole time. And now that there are worldwide rebellions, which if left alone are certain to eventually bring me down, the need for a foil has grown exponentially. If I am to win back control of this world, I will need a world threat power to conveniently wipe out my foes and be blamed for their deaths. And that world threat will be you. So, what of that plan did you know?"

Victor swallowed hard.

"Symon once mentioned the LO-EC energy suppressor, and briefly discussed his work using LO-EC energy for healing purposes. I was not familiar with anything else," he said.

"Good," Spidre replied, and signaled once more to an engineer. Commands were input into the control panel. The cylinder spun around again and when it stopped moving, its front door swung open with a hydraulic hiss, revealing a confined, windowless interior that was barely large enough to fit two people.

"Now, get in and begin the process of becoming—"

"No," Victor growled as he interrupted Spidre.

"I was not asking!" Spidre bellowed. Victor remained motionless.

"I am commanding you to get in that apparatus!" Spidre continued.

Victor took one step forward but as he stared into the KROE the chamber seemed to get smaller and smaller. Even from this distance, he felt panicked and suffocated thinking about being in a space that small and enclosed.

"No…" Victor whimpered as he stopped forward progress again and a tear rolled down his face. His twitches and breathing grew more intense.

Spidre threw an angry glare at the lead engineer, who seemed baffled at what he was witnessing. Spidre pushed him aside and walked up to the right of Victor. He extended his energy blade from his left hand and swung it to within an inch of Victor's throat.

"Get in the KROE now or I will kill you where you stand!" Spidre screamed. With a barely-in-control right hand, Victor gently pushed Spidre's arm to the side and with all his effort swung another foot forward. He felt his heart pounding in his chest and his vision had gone blurry from tears, but the sight of the KROE was burned into his brain. Another step forward and his head started spinning. Another step and the dizziness was so bad that Victor wasn't sure he could continue to stand. Another step and Victor could feel his brain being torn apart. His twitching was now uncontrollable and the single thought in his head was of that terrifying chamber now ten feet in front of him. He screamed as he took another step forward, and what started as an incoherent roar slowly turned back into words.

"Nooooo!" Victor finally got out as he threw up his arms and air bursts flew forward. The KROE was obliterated, instantly becoming thousands of pieces of projectile metal that flew into every surface. Victor, Spidre, and all the engineers were littered with cuts as metal flew around the room. Metal pierced through control panels and walls and everything started to spark, hiss, or outright explode.

"I will fucking kill you!" Spidre screamed and extended his other energy blade from his right palm. Victor turned and the frenzied look in his eyes sent chills through Spidre. Victor roared again and unleashed a barrage of air bursts. Spidre brought his blades up and sliced through the air as the burst neared, dispersing just enough of it to keep him stationary.

"We've got to get out of here!" the lead engineer yelled, drawing Victor's attention. Victor unleashed an air burst and the lead engineer was thrown backward so hard that his spine audibly cracked in half as it hit a control panel. Others in the room began to scream in terror and Victor targeted them one by one. The attack was over in moments, but by the end of it, all of the engineers were dead after being either thrown through the air or having their internal organs exploded by the force of the impact. Spidre launched one of his blades at Victor but Victor's reflexes kicked in. He dodged out of the way and ran straight at Spidre. Spidre put his left blade in front of his body for defense and readied the right blade to strike. Spidre's range was longer, and as Victor entered striking distance Spidre brought his right blade around for the kill. But somewhere in the back of Victor's frayed mind, the training he'd done with Nadine still broke through. He saw Spidre's attack coming and dodged to the outside of the swing. Spidre immediately brought his arm back in the direction it came and made contact, but Victor had gotten so close that the blow was a conventional elbow to the head rather than a deadly swing of an energy blade. Victor ate the blow and threw a jab of his own just under Spidre's armpit.

Spidre was no novice at hand-to-hand combat. He knew he was outmatched on speed but had a massive size advantage. He took the opportunity this close-quarter-combat provided, Turning and bringing both blades down towards Victor. Victor reached up and grabbed both arms at the wrist. Victor pushed hard against Spidre's downward pressure, and Spidre met the force in-kind. They stood and struggled against each other's opposing strength. Growls and grunts escaped from both their mouths as each tried to get an advantage over the other. Finally, it was Spidre who won. Victor's right elbow buckled from the pressure, and he fell to the ground with Spidre on top of him. Spidre rained down punches but could only get glancing blows. Any time he pulled back to unleash an energy blade, Victor would push that hand away. Eventually, Victor was able to throw both of Spidre's hands away at once, and before Spidre could bring an arm back to defend Victor threw a two-handed palm thrust into Spidre's chest. Spidre was thrown off his prey and Victor spun to his feet.

Victor threw an air burst as Spidre threw an energy blade and the two projectile attacks met in midair and obliterated one another. Victor let out yet another guttural yell as he charged at Spidre a second time. Spidre set himself up in the same position as last round. This time, as Victor drew near, Spidre switched stances and stepped toward Victor while also thrusting his right energy blade forward. The unconventional move caught Victor off-guard. He dodged, but too late, and Spidre's blade pierced completely through Victor's left shoulder. Spidre expected Victor to scream and try to pull his body off of the blade. Victor instead gritted his teeth through the pain and stood his ground, and for a millisecond, Spidre was aware the fight was over. Victor threw up his right arm and unleashed an airburst at Spidre at point-blank-range. The air burst landed directly in Spidre's face and ripped his head clean from his torso. His energy blades immediately dissipated, and his body slumped to the ground.

Victor didn't even take a moment to acknowledge the victory. If anything, the fact that he now had no singular target made his behavior even more wild and chaotic. He threw airbursts continuously around the room. Floors, ceilings, and support beams crumbled. He darted through the holes in the walls and ran around the compound destroying anything and anyone in sight. A hurricane had been unleashed within the San Francisco compound, and there was absolutely nothing that could stand in its way.

As Victor made his way through the building, an occasional soldier or engineer would be fleeing, and they immediately became a crumpled mess plastered to a wall. Occasionally a soldier was brave or stupid enough to try and take a shot, but they had no chance. Under normal circumstances, Victor was too fast for a bullet he could see coming. Now, with his brain running on instincts and reflexes alone, bullets might as well have been soft lobs.

After dozens of air bursts had been thrown, the west-most side of the structure had finally had enough. The walls and floors collapsed and laid out a path of rubble for Victor to sprint down. It was at this point he finally heard the alarms blaring throughout the entire compound, but he did not acknowledge them. As he made it to ground level, he turned to see that the outer wall had continued to crumble for another 30 or 40 feet to the left of the rubble ramp, exposing the giant room where he had fought both Spidre and his friends. The room was now full of vehicles that had been disabled in the assault, all being worked on by various automated machines. Victor ran through the opening and alternated between throwing air burst and ripping machines apart with his bare hands. The air bursts effortlessly tore through the metal occupants of the room and buried into the already compromised walls and support structures. As Victor made it about halfway through the room, the entire building started to groan. Another few seconds and the ceiling above began to bow. Another second later and the roar of the collapsing upper floors was unmistakable. Victor threw an air burst at the far wall and sprinted through it just as the building fell around him.

Outside, he caught sight of what looked to be the last soldiers in the compound, organizing into rows to open fire on him. He came to a stop and allowed the dust cloud of the collapsing building to envelope him. The soldiers opened fire into the shroud and Victor darted out to the left away from their fire. They tried to reposition and follow his trajectory, but they were hopelessly slow. Victor arced towards them and threw air bursts non-stop. Many soldiers went flying and those that didn't fell into a disorganized mess. When the gunfire ceased for a moment, Victor careened head-on into the group and let off an air burst with both arms, spinning as he did so. The peacekeepers closest to him were ripped off their feet and flung in every direction imaginable. A handful the air burst had missed ran at him, and one by one he ripped them apart or pummeled them into the dirt. As the last head hit the ground, Victor looked around and saw others running away, either towards the last remaining vehicles scattered around the compound or out into the open desert. One by one Victor caught them, some leaving the ground via air burst, others becoming red stains on the cracked earth.

On the outskirts of the compound, Victor caught up with the last living human, an exhausted engineer who was barely still on her feet. Victor grabbed her by the back of her neck and threw her back towards the compound. Victor saw the compound's smaller buildings still standing, and his rage built anew. He charged at the closest edifice and unleashed air bursts as he did so. Walls crumbled away and Victor raced through the hole he had made. He continued to throw air bursts all around him as he brought down walls to reach the other side of the building. He broke through to the outside again, and behind him he heard the now all-too-familiar sound of the building coming down. He saw another building standing in front of him and repeated the process of bringing it down. Then he did it again, and again, and again until one final building remained. It was the smallest building on the compound, a single-story storage shed of some kind. He crashed through the wall and threw two air bursts to his sides, and then one more above his head. The building exploded outward around him.

Having no more targets for his rage, Victor began throwing air bursts at the largest nearby pieces of debris. He continued until there was so little left, his bursts were flying off into nothingness. It was only then, surrounded by quiet desolation, that some semblance of cognitive thought returned to his mind.

If they… come back… he thought. He turned back to the pile of rocks that was once Spidre's main facility and began digging through the rubble looking for bodies.

CHAPTER THIRTY-FIVE

Nadine and Edgar's eyes darted back and forth from Victor above them to the pile of bodies in front of them. Spidre's headless torso was easy to spot, it was still a large and looming form amongst the smaller frames of the engineers. Eventually, near the bottom of the pile, Edgar noticed Spidre's head as well. The eyes and nose were caved in from a blow, but the beard and jawline were unmistakable. He pointed it out to Nadine and the sight finally prompted further conversation.

"You did it, Victor, you killed him," Nadine said. "Did you put them all here so we would know you're alone? Does this mean—"

"Too small…" Victor growled as he interrupted Nadine.

"What-what does that mean?" Edgar said.

"I couldn't… I couldn't…" Victor replied.

"Something is wrong," Nadine said to Edgar.

"Victor, we figured out what happened," Nadine said. "We know you were under Spidre's control and weren't acting of your own free will. Please come with us, you need help."

"No, no, no, no," Victor replied.

"Victor!" Edgar yelled. "We are your friends! I am your friend!

We will figure this out together and get you better. Just come down and come with us.”

Tears started to roll down Victor’s face.

“I have to kill you. He said to kill you,” Victor said as he pointed at Spidre.

“He’s dead, Victor!” Edgar yelled. “The fighting is over, and it’s because of you. You did it! You! Did! It! His orders don’t mean shit now!”

“I must follow my commands…” Victor replied through gritted teeth and clenched fists.

“Fight it, Victor!” Nadine yelled as she took a defensive posture. “You already proved you’re stronger than this fucker, don’t let him win! Don’t give him dominion over you like this!”

“Leave!” Victor screeched, making Nadine and Edgar jump.

“If I don’t know where you are, I don’t have to kill you,” Victor continued in a softer tone.

“Fuck that shit! What, we just avoid you for the rest of our lives while your brain gets more and more messed up? We go back to hiding while you waste away? Fuck that! Fuck that!” Edgar screamed with tears welling up in his eyes.

Now, knowing that Spidre was out of the equation, new strategies started playing in Nadine’s head. Being able to team up against Victor without worrying about another lethal opponent afforded some opportunities she hadn’t previously considered viable.

“This ends one of four ways, and us leaving without you is not one of them,” Nadine said through clenched teeth. “One: You leave here with us of your own free will. Two: We knock you out and keep you out until we can fix you. Three: You kill the both of us right here and now. Or four: We kill you. I really, really do not want it to be either of the last two.”

Victor hung his head and clasped his hands behind it. He rocked back on forth and occasionally grunted. The rocking became more and more severe and the grunts turned into yelps. Then, the rocking stopped, he pulled his head in as close to his chest as it could possibly go and let out a yell filled with emotion. At the end of the yell, it turned into words.

"I'm sorry," he uttered before leaping from his perch on the rubble and throwing an air burst down at Nadine and Edgar.

Edgar dodged right and Nadine dodged left, and the second Victor landed he turned straight for Nadine.

"Try to knock him out!" Nadine yelled to Edgar as she activated the energy in her hands and feet and squared up just in time to block Victor's left hook. She threw a jab of her own that only got a glancing blow as Victor ducked under it. Victor threw a jab in reply as he ducked but even with his speed, Nadine's fighting experience allowed her to predict the move and get out of the way in time. By now Edgar was getting close to joining the action, and when Victor noticed he immediately backed away from Nadine, threw an air burst at Edgar to keep him at bay, then went back to his hand-to-hand assault. This same pattern happened several times over, and it became clear to Nadine that her earlier prediction had been correct. Any time Victor felt threatened, his speed allowed him to disengage from the fight and re-strategize. If she was going to get Edgar back into the action, she needed to try something less orthodox.

Nadine deactivated the blue energy at her hands and feet and waited for Victor to strike. When he came in with a left, Nadine attempted to step around him and grapple him to the ground. She had barely covered grapples with Victor, but he was still able to respond. He rolled his shoulder to throw her, but Nadine countered with a headlock as she was tossed, and both of them fell to the ground. They rolled around in the dirt as Nadine desperately held on to Victor while Victor wailed on her with ferocious punches and kicks. Nadine held her grip and Edgar dove at Victor with his left fist extended and made direct contact right in between Victor's eyes. A loud thud echoed off the rubble due to the blow, but despite that, Victor seemed dazed for only a moment before shaking it off and wriggling free of Nadine. He swung back to his feet and darted away from the both of them.

"Keep him distracted," Nadine said to Edgar as she took to the air. Victor kept his distance and continued to throw air bursts at Edgar, but Edgar was able to use his energy blades to slice through and dissipate them enough to not cause damage. Eventually, Victor got tired of the stalemate and ran towards Edgar. The punch Edgar had delivered earlier was about as powerful a blow as he could muster, so he knew a knockout wasn't an option for him. Still, he hoped that enough injuries could incapacitate Victor without him dying and focused his attacks on Victor's extremities. But landing a hit on someone with that much speed was difficult, and Victor's arms and legs were the fastest parts of all. Surprisingly, Edgar's all-out offensive push kept Victor on his heels. Edgar's size and reach advantage kept Victor far enough away that he couldn't take advantage of the openings when Edgar swung. Edgar kept going for small, quick flick-of-the-wrist attacks that didn't leave big openings for Victor to come in on, and Victor once again got frustrated. Victor disengaged and backed out again and as he did, he fell right into Nadine's trap.

Nadine found the largest chunk of debris she could possibly move and kicked it with the energy in her feet activated. The chunk of concrete went sailing through the air right at the spot where Victor retreated to. Victor threw an air burst at the hunk of rock and rather than stop its trajectory, the hit caused the concrete to explode into thousands of tiny pieces that continued towards him. Victor covered his face as the pebbles pelted him, and Edgar seized on the opportunity. He ran forward and lunged at Victor, wrapping hands around Victor's entire torso. Edgar held him down and Nadine pounced on top as well. She pummeled Victor's face with hits as he thrashed around trying to escape the grip. Finally, he managed to get free and slammed both hands into Nadine's chest to throw her off. Again, he shook his head a couple of times and was back on his feet, still conscious and ready to fight.

"I have two more tricks I want to try," Nadine said.

"Right," Edgar responded.

Nadine took to the air again, but this time Victor wasn't losing track of her. He alternated throwing air bursts up at her and over at Edgar, keeping them both at bay. This time, Nadine was trying to knock Victor out by dive bombing a punch directly down onto him, but there was no opening. She circled in the sky in one direction and, realizing what was happening, Edgar circled in the opposite direction. Eventually the two of them were on opposite sides of Victor, and by continually slowing down and speeding up, Victor had trouble keeping pace with them. Eventually he was in too awkward of a position to keep throwing air bursts at Nadine and had to readjust. Edgar pounced on the opportunity and charged in, but Victor was too quick. He turned and threw an airburst that swept Edgar's legs out from under him. Edgar went tumbling head over heels and as he did so, Nadine dove in for an attack, hoping to also seize an opening while Victor was distracted. Once again, Victor's speed proved too much, he turned and quickly threw an air burst upwards. His aim was slightly high, but the edge of the burst still caught Nadine in the face and whipped her around through the air. For a moment Nadine thought she was going to be the one to lose consciousness, but she was able to shake it off.

Nadine's face throbbed. She felt a warm sensation on her lips and chin and reached up to feel it. It was blood pouring out of her nostrils, her nose was broken. She only had one other trick up her sleeve, and if it didn't work, then only Edgar's failsafe plan was left. She dove at Victor, and he saw her coming, but it did not matter. He threw airbursts up at her and she continued on her path towards him. She protected her face with her energized hands, but the impact from the air bursts was fierce. Blow after blow hit her hands and arms and she felt bone after bone snap as the hits landed. Despite this, enough of the air burst power was being deflected that she could continue down towards Victor.

Edgar got back to his feet and bided his time, waiting for the time to charge. And when he thought Nadine was close enough, he went after Victor with both blades drawn. Victor saw Edgar out of the corner of his eye and turned his focus away from Nadine. He threw two airbursts at Edgar and Edgar dodged them. The distraction was brief, but it was enough. Nadine reached Victor and fought through the pain in her arms to wrap Victor up and get him off the ground. Victor again tried to wriggle free, but Nadine kept her grip. She turned for the largest debris pile and ducked her head as she plowed Victor and herself into it with full force. A thunderous boom leapt into the air from the impact, and rocks and dust flew everywhere.

After several additional moments of loud noise from the rubble shifting, the sounds started to dull. Fifteen seconds passed, and the compound went virtually silent. All Edgar could hear was his own heavy breathing. He ran towards the site of the impact and as he got close, he saw through the dust Victor climbing out of the hole, shaking his head violently.

"Holy shit there is no stopping this guy," Edgar thought. Somehow Victor seemed even less normal than before. Victor's eyes seemed completely devoid of thought. His glances now seemed animalistic or instinctual. Edgar was worried about Victor turning back towards Nadine in the hole, so he screamed as loudly as he could while charging at Victor with both energy blades drawn.

"Victor, enough already!" Edgar screamed as he approached. Victor didn't listen. At this point Edgar wasn't even sure if Victor could comprehend what he was saying. Before the fight, Victor's mind was already clearly fraying, and now he had taken multiple severe hits to the head on top of it.

Victor threw a few air bursts, but Edgar sliced through them and kept coming. Victor was still against the rubble pile and somewhat cornered, so he stopped the long-range assault and ran towards Edgar instead.

"Victor, please don't make me do this," Edgar pleaded with tears in his eyes but again, he couldn't tell if his words even connected. Victor again tried getting inside but had trouble because of Edgar's reach. Victor flipped and ducked and dodged but Edgar kept his wits about him and kept his movements small and fast. Edgar's quick strikes kept Victor on the defensive, but they weren't fast enough to land, and Edgar was getting exhausted. He was almost certain that the Victor he knew wasn't in operation right now, and that this new Victor wasn't going to stop fighting until it was physically impossible for him to continue. Edgar had to end this.

Edgar withdrew his energy blades but kept his hands up, and hoped Victor would take the bait and try to get inside of Edgar's reach. He did, and when Victor was a step closer Edgar slightly changed the angle of his hand and reactivated his right blade.

The energy shot from in between his fingers and pierced through Victor's shoulder in almost the exact same spot where Spidre had stabbed him. And just like in that fight, Victor didn't jump back or try to get free, but instead threw an air burst at point blank range. Unlike Spidre, Edgar saw it coming, but it was still far too fast and close. Edgar leaned his head to the left and it avoided the blow, but the entire right side of his torso took the full force of the hit with nothing impeding it. Edgar felt his right side completely collapse as he was thrown backwards. As his blade came out of Victor's shoulder, he used every ounce of concentration he had left to slightly change the angle of his hand, and as his vision started going black, he could just barely make out the sight of his energy blade leaping away from his hand and piercing Victor's chest. Both fighters collapsed to the ground and stopped moving.

CHAPTER THIRTY-SIX

"I'm not sure I understand what the plan was," Alison said.

"It wasn't really a plan, per se," Nadine replied. "Just ideas of what could surprise someone with lightning quick reflexes and who knew all of our moves."

It had been about nine days since the fight with Victor, and Nadine and Edgar were back in New Orleans. Nadine had recovered enough and mourned enough to finally give Alison a rundown of what happened.

"Ages ago, when we all first met, Symon did a checkup on each of us to see what our potential capabilities and weaknesses were. Since Edgar's powers were similar to Spidre's in appearance, he of course asked if he could one day learn to shoot his blades off as a projectile the same way Spidre did. Symon said he could not, and that Spidre must have gone through some insane procedure for that to be possible."

"I guess we know what that procedure was, now," Alison replied. Nadine nodded.

"At the time, Symon mentioned that for Edgar to do something like that, he'd have to sustain a severe enough hit that the entire

LO-EC conduit network in his arm was severed all at once. Symon told us about it intending it as a cautionary note, that a hit like that would very likely kill Edgar. But that's my Edgar, turning his pain into a guaranteed victory."

As she said this, Nadine grabbed Edgar's hand and smiled. Edgar was awake and listening, and he smiled back.

"I'm stubborn that way," Edgar said very weak and raspy, then immediately went into a coughing fit.

"Hey! You are recovering from a collapsed lung! No talking!" Alison scolded him. Edgar nodded as the coughing subsided.

"So, you took a direct hit from Victor knowing it would do this much damage, all so you could surprise him with a shot unexpectedly firing from your hand?" Alison asked.

Edgar nodded.

"Well, I can say that you are, without a doubt, the bravest and stupidest fucker I have ever met," Alison said.

"That's why I love him. My courageous dummy," Nadine said as she stared into Edgar's eyes.

"Wow, I haven't heard you call him dummy in forever," they heard from the other side of Edgar. Everyone glanced over to see Naren's eyes squinting as they got used to the lighting.

"You're awake!" Nadine screamed as she dove over Edgar and wrapped her hands around her brother.

"Whoa. How long was I out for?" Naren asked.

"Weeks. You've woken up a couple times in the past few days but not fully cognizant like this," Alison replied as she walked around Edgar to Naren's beside.

"I know that voice," Naren said, his eyesight still blurry.

"Alison? We're in New Orleans… right, I remember now…" he continued, and as his memories came back his head sank.

"I'm so sorry, Naren," Nadine said. Naren sniffled in response.

"At least, thanks to you and Edgar, that traitorous fucker isn't still out there plotting who knows what," Naren said.

"There have been a lot of developments since the last time you were conscious." Nadine said. "We can talk about them more when the wounds aren't so fresh."

"I want to talk about them now," Naren said. Alison and Nadine exchanged worried looks.

"Please, Nadine. I need the distraction."

Nadine nodded firmly, then proceeded to fill Naren in on everything that had happened: Why Victor betrayed them, how they figured out that Victor was being controlled, and how Spidre and Victor finally met their ends.

"…All things considered, I got off easy, just broken bones all over my arms and face. Edgar has multiple shattered ribs, damage to every bone and soft tissue connection in his shoulder, and his lung collapsed. And that is nothing still compared to the extensive bullet wounds and crushing damage you took. Both of you will be laid up for months," Nadine concluded.

"Fuck," Naren said in response. "How many people did Victor kill in Halifax?"

"We don't know yet," Nadine said "They aren't exactly on speaking terms with anyone right now and I can't blame them. But it must be hundreds, maybe thousands, and surely some or all of the LO-ECs are among them."

"Fuck… Fuck…" Naren said as he stared directly ahead.

"But did we ever get concrete proof that Victor was being controlled by Spidre?" he eventually continued. "That it wasn't just betrayal? Everything you mentioned was your own theory and some light evidence from your conversation with a very distressed Victor."

"Alison and some of her followers took the TCT to do a salvage operation at—"

"You took the Trans-Continental Transit?!" Naren exclaimed before wincing in pain.

"No yelling!" Alison scolded.

"They can do that now, Naren. We all can. Spidre is dead and the world government is in chaos," Nadine replied.

"Right, right," Naren said.

"I wanted someone to get back there immediately before anyone realized what had happened and looted the compound, so Alison and the congregation did a salvage operation. They found the central database where the research files were kept. It confirmed a whole host of things, including that Victor was under Spidre's control, and that the LO-EC energy suppressor that Symon developed was the delivery mechanism for the mind control tech."

"What else did it confirm?" Naren asked.

"Well, to start with, it confirmed that the mind control wasn't Spidre's only secret,"

"There was more?!" Naren exclaimed and again immediately regretted it as waves of pain coursed through him.

"This is your last warning. Another outburst and I'm ending this conversation for your own well-being," Alison said.

"I'm sorry," Naren said.

"Spidre developed an apparatus called the KROE, the Kinetic Reorganizer of Organic Energy. And while the details were light regarding the mind control tech and how it was developed, there were extensive files on development of the KROE. They killed some kid who had powers like Sera and the KROE used his power to give any LO-EC user a significant upgrade. It was how Spidre got his superpowered abilities, and I think it also led to his downfall."

"How do you mean?" Naren asked?

"The data logs said he wanted to create a LO-EC user with unbelievable power, then use the mind control to send them out into cities to wreak havoc. Then Spidre's regime would swoop in and kill the new threat, but all the while the threat was under his control. He intended to keep the world afraid of LO-ECs and continuing to support him. Unfortunately, the LO-EC he took control over was claustrophobic, and the KROE was a tiny, windowless cylinder."

"Is it really that simple? The mind control couldn't overcome a fear of small spaces?" Naren asked.

"I just don't see another explanation," Nadine replied. "Victor's head was all sorts of messed up when we last saw him, and he had destroyed the entire compound and killed Spidre. The only thing that makes sense is that his phobia caused him to fight the effect of the mind control, and in doing so it ripped his brain apart."

"I get it, but was this thing really so small that it would cause that level of fear?" Naren asked.

"Yes," Nadine replied.

"How do you know?" Naren asked.

"Because… of the data files…" Nadine replied, not wanting to discuss further details.

"Nadine, what aren't you telling me?" Naren said.

"Something I don't think you can handle right now," Nadine responded. Naren glared at her and continued to do so as Nadine summoned the courage to keep talking.

"The last research file uploaded discussed experiments they were conducting on Symon and Sera using the KROE. For some reason, Spidre thought it could bring them back to life, but it failed. The KROE did change Symon's LO-EC system and might have also changed Sera's but they were still dead. When the experiment failed, Spidre ordered them cremated. The very last research log entry was from the lead engineer confirming completion of this task."

Naren went pale and wide-eyed.

"He took everything. That fucker took everything. He didn't even leave a fucking body to bury!?" Naren screamed and then once again doubled over in pain. Alison refrained from scolding him again; she could see that the conversation was over.

The rest of the night was filled with a lot of tears and cursing. Eventually, everyone fell asleep and didn't wake up until very late morning the next day. Naren was the last to wake up, and as he did so Alison came over with food.

"Alison, now that the local forces are gone and the world government is practically non-existent, what do you think of building a memorial to Sera somewhere outside?" Naren asked. "I know she spent her whole life here, but I just feel like something dedicated to her memory shouldn't be kept underground, you know?"

"I would say it's a great idea. So good in fact that we already thought of it and have some artists working on concepts now," Alison responded, getting the faintest of smiles out of Naren.

"We also thought about doing a memorial for Symon here as well," Nadine said as she joined the conversation. "His hideout in San Diego has been bombed to dust, his original roots in Salt Lake City are also gone, and the only other tie he has anywhere is to May in Chicago, but not to Chicago itself."

"I mean, I guess it works considering there aren't other standout options," Naren said. "What about Victor? Actually, where is Victor even being kept?"

"We cleared out one of the smaller food storage areas in the sub-basement and put him in there," Alison said. "It is very cold in those rooms, so we thought that'd be the best place to have him while we figure out what to do."

"That worked? Like, he's still, you know?" Naren asked.

"I had my doubts, too, but it seemed to work fine. No decay, not even rigor mortis," Alison replied.

"Good, but we should still make a decision quickly." Naren said.

"There were really only two options I could think of. Either we bury him here near the memorials for Symon and Sera, or we bury him out at his old campsite in the woods," Nadine said.

"He built that campsite with his parents, right?" Naren asked.

"I don't remember if it was that exact site, but he went to that forest with them all the time when he was a kid," Nadine replied.

"Maybe that might be more appropriate then. His only connection here at the garden is us. The campsite has connections both to us and to his family."

"Ok. Campsite it is," Alison said. "If you get me the coordinates, I'll arrange for him to be brought out there and buried."

"When he is laid to rest, I want to be there," Naren said.

"Me, too," Nadine said.

"Me, too," Edgar said in his low raspy voice, and then immediately entered another coughing fit.

Alison stayed silent for a few moments as she thought it over.

"As long as we can get a military personnel transport to bring you all, we should be able to get everyone out there. I'll work on it," Alison said.

Over the course of the next day, Alison's congregation searched the military's now-defunct storage facilities and found a personnel carrier that was in working order. They wrapped Victor in white cloth, loaded him onto the floor of the transport, and tied him down near the back. With a significant amount of assistance and pain, Edgar and Naren were able to climb into the transport from a side entrance. Alison and several members of her sect joined them while Nadine led the way on the elcycle. The military transport was much slower than their usual means of transportation, and by the time they made it to the campsite, it was late afternoon. Alison's group dug a grave near Victor's old lean-to, and then they slowly and carefully lowered Victor's body into the grave with the cloth still wrapped around him. Alison led a short prayer, then her members began filling the hole back in.

"I know that what we've done has made the world better," Naren said as he leaned heavily on Nadine for support. "I know we wanted Spidre gone, and we succeeded. I know LO-ECs can now live without fear and that all of humanity has its first chance in decades to heal."

Naren stopped talking briefly as he choked back tears.

"But a part of me can't help but want to trade all of that to have Symon and Victor alive, and Sera back here in my arms. I'm sure that makes me selfish but—"

"No," Alison interrupted. "It makes you human."